With Every Breath

By Ruth O'Neil

Scripture quotations were taken from the Holy Bible, New International Version ®. Copyright 1973, 1978, 1984 International Bible Society. Used by permission of Zondervan.

Published by:
Books for Future Generations

Cover design by Ruth O'Neil

ISBN: 978-1-7369266-5-9

Chapter One

"Come on! You can stay for one more drink," Ethan begged through slurred words and twisting one of her brown curls around his finger. "Your hair color exactly matches your eyes."

Addie laughed. "I have a feeling I should go." Addie's words were no less slurred. And she was confused. She never wanted to leave the bar this early or in her own car. Typically, she had to call a taxi to pick her up from where she had landed for the night and take her back to the bar to pick up her car. But something was definitely pulling her away this night. The smell of cigarette smoke and beer were getting to her tonight. "Send me a text," Addie said as she fell into the driver's seat of her car. "Woop!" she laughed as she slid a little too far to the right, the shift stick stabbing her in the thigh.

"I will," Ethan promised.

She hadn't gotten more than a mile down the road when her phone pinged with a text notification.

As promised.

Addie couldn't help but laugh out loud at the text Ethan sent. Honestly, she wasn't sure if the text was truly that funny or if she maybe should not have had that last drink. When she'd had a little too much alcohol, she got punchy. She laughed at a lot of things that weren't funny. When she was trying to get the attention of some new man, Addie had a habit of laughing hysterically at everything he said. The alcohol just made it worse. She may have been a little punchy, but drunk, no. Since she liked to be in control, Addie never let her drinking go that far. Unless of course, one asked Carrie's opinion. Carrie was Addie's younger sister who never did one wrong thing one day of her life. Carrie had a lot of opinions Addie didn't share. As sisters, they shared DNA, yes. But opinions, no. It didn't matter anyway. Carrie lived on the other side of the country now and was mostly out of Addie's life. Thankfully.

Addie started up her car and backed slowly out of her parking spot. She knew she wouldn't have any problem driving the five miles home. All she'd had to drink were wine coolers, and they hardly contained any alcohol. Oh, and the shot of tequila, but that had been at the beginning of the night.

Her phone dinged, signaling another text. Keeping one hand on the wheel and one eye on the road, the other hand and eye held her phone while she read the text. This time Ethan sent an inappropriate picture along with inappropriate words. This made Addie laugh uncontrollably, making her swerve just the littlest bit. Quickly, she swerved back into her lane.

Headlights from an oncoming car suddenly appeared in her vision.

"What are you doing on my side of the road?" she shouted, adding a few expletives before the metal on metal impact and the sound of breaking glass crashed into her life.

She felt what she thought was the airbag stealing the breath out of her. Addie panicked when she realized she couldn't inhale enough to fill her lungs. It was like she almost couldn't breathe at all. The last thing she saw was that it was actually the steering wheel and the dashboard pressing the life out of her, not the airbags. Oh, how her chest hurt!

"Can you feel that?"

Toddler Addie looked up at her mother with a smile. Her hand was on her mom's protruding belly. Addie did feel something. She didn't speak much yet, but a smile came when she felt the movement she was waiting for.

"That's your little sister. She's coming soon."

Being so young, Addie didn't understand this fully. She had just known that Mama made Addie sit next to her instead of on her lap recently. There wasn't much room in Mama's lap anymore. And maybe Addie was a little jealous.

∞ ∞ ∞

Addie tried to move her head, but it was held down fast. What had brought about that memory? One Addie didn't even truly remember. And what made her think of her little sister? Oh, yeah. Carrie's voice had been in Addie's head, reprimanding her for drinking too much.

"I'm not surprised about this one." A voice she almost recognized came drifting in on the air she wished she could inhale deeply.

"You know her then?"

"Sort of. We've had a business relationship of sorts, if you know what I mean."

"Smells like she's been drinking."

"Yup. I'm sure she has."

Addie couldn't say anything, although she wanted to put these people in their place. Why were they talking about her like she couldn't hear them? And where was she? It was so dark she couldn't see anything.

She still felt as if she was gasping for breath, so she knew she needed to relax. Attempting to inhale deeply, Addie allowed her mind to drift back in time in her memories. They fast-forwarded to when baby Carrie came home for the first time. She was so tiny, even to Addie, who at fifteen months older really wasn't that much bigger.

Addie remembered Carrie had cried a lot and that her parents were always taking care of Carrie and not leaving them much time for Addie. At the time, Addie probably didn't recognize anything as being strange since she was so young, but as she got older she certainly did. She spent more time playing alone while Carrie cried for hours on end. There was nothing wrong with her lungs! And here Addie was now, struggling for each breath.

Finally, Carrie grew out of it, but by then it was too late. Addie was independent and didn't need anyone, not even her parents, and especially not her little sister. Used to being held so much at first, Carrie still enjoyed the comfort of her mother's arms. Addie could remember Mama carrying Carrie around in a sling on the front of her body. It kept Carrie from crying, and Mama got stuff done. Addie was quiet and left alone for the most part. At least that's how Addie remembered it.

"I can't breathe," she thought she heard herself say.

"Don't worry. We're taking care of you."

In the next moment, someone covered her mouth with a mask that made it feel a little easier to breathe.

Addie felt herself drifting off into a world made up of memories. She allowed herself to fall into the inviting sleep.

"Look at this!" Grandma Marjie was pointing at yet another painting for little Addie to take note of.

Addie looked up as instructed. It was a pretty painting of a barnyard, but something about it made it look special, although Addie was too little to put her finger on it. She gripped Grandma Marjie's hand tighter. She wasn't sure if that was because she didn't want to get lost in the huge art museum or because there was something about the artwork that thrilled her to the tips of her toes. Addie could not stop smiling; a huge grin made her cheeks hurt. Addie may only have been about five years old, but she knew she wanted to be an artist when she grew up. She had always loved to color and draw pictures, but this trip with Grandma Marjie sealed that deal.

Mom's parents lived far away, and Addie didn't get to see them too often, but it was always an amazing time when she did. Grandma and Grandpa lived in the big city, and there was always so much to do, and they made everything seem like the most fun.

∞ ∞ ∞

Her dreams shifted one into another, a blurry conglomerate of pictures from the deep recesses of Addie's mind. This time in her memories, she and Carrie were playing in their room with their shared dollhouse.

∞ ∞ ∞

"I want to be the mom!" Addie shouted.

"No, it's my turn. Remember what Mom said?"

"I don't care what Mom said. I'm going to be the mom."

Carrie narrowed her eyes and sat back on her rear. "You want to be the mom because you know you're a bad kid."

"What?" It was the first time Carrie ever said anything mean and derogatory to Addie.

"Yeah. Dad told me you were so bad they wanted to have a better baby."

Addie had no words. Was it true? Did Dad really say that? Finally, she spouted out, "You cried all the time, and Mommy couldn't ever put you down."

11

"She didn't want to put me down because she loves me more than she loves you."

Addie stood up, her face flaming red with anger. She threw down the mom doll she was holding. "Fine! You can be the mom. I never want to play with you again!" She stomped out of the room and went to play in the back yard by herself. That may have been the first moment Addie realized she hated having a sister.

Visions shifted to another memory. Addie was sitting at the dining room table, coloring furiously. Even in her dreams, Addie could feel the anger coming off her younger self.

"Stupid!" Addie said as she threw down a colored pencil with another broken tip. These were her special colored pencils Grandma Marjie had bought after their museum trip, and Addie wanted to make them last as long as possible. It was the last gift she would ever receive from her.

Addie tried staying in the lines like Grandma Marjie had shown her. She was good at that, but she was coloring so hard because of her anger, and she kept breaking the tips of her beautiful pencils. Soon, there would not be any left in the box. Grabbing another pencil, she noticed something. There were more pencils in the box than there were at her last grab. How could that happen?

When she looked up, she saw Carrie sitting across the table from her. Carrie hadn't been there before. Now, she was picking up Addie's pencils after they broke and was

painstakingly sharpening them to a nice point once again.,
and making the pencils extremely short.

"What are you doing? You're using up all my pencils!"

Carrie shrank into herself a little bit. "I was just trying to
help you. I wanted to sharpen them for you after they
broke."

Addie snatched the sharpener out of Carrie's hands and
scooped up all the colored pencils, putting them back in the
box. "Well, you're ruining them!"

"I'm sad, too." Huge tears dropped out of her eyes and
rolled down her cheeks.

Addie knew she was talking about the news of their
grandparents' death, but she ignored that.

"I'm not sad; I'm angry! Leave my stuff alone!"

Addie tossed and turned in a restless sleep, not sure
of what brought her grandparents to mind. They had
died in a car accident not long after that museum trip.
Addie knew they had always loved her. She always felt
safe with them, even though she was so young when
they passed away. One thing she did know was that
after they died, her life was never the same. Many days
since then, Addie felt as if they were the only ones who
ever loved her for who she was. Even though their

deaths were years ago now, their memories had never faded. Addie could still smell Grandma Marjie's perfume, a fragrance similar to baby powder. Surprisingly, Addie could still see Grandma Margie's face. She and Addie had matching brown hair and eyes, except that Grandma's hair was starting to get some gray mixed in.

Beeping pulled Addie out of her semi-conscious memory snippet. When she tried to open her eyes, blinding lights seemed to be pointing directly into her face. It was better to keep her eyes closed. The sound of continuous beeps reached her ears, and she still felt as if she could not take a deep breath. She heard several different voices all talking over each other, but she couldn't understand much of the chaotic conversation. Until the one.

"We need another nurse in here! Call that new guy!"

In another moment, Addie heard, "What can I do?" The male voice sent familiar echoes through Addie's throbbing head.

"Grab the anesthesia."

Nothing

"Did you hear me?" It was the voice with authority.

"Yes. I'm sorry. I know her."

"Can you do this?"

"Yes."

There was a lot of scuffling, as if someone was rearranging furniture.

"Make sure she's out. This is going to be a long surgery. Close to twelve hours for the double transplant."

Out of nowhere, a clear, plastic mask rested on the lower part of Addie's face, covering her mouth. The air coming into her body offered her rest, sweet rest. She felt no pain and was dreaming in seconds. She felt strange, detached. She was there, yet not there. It was as if she were watching an old home video of her life. Her dreams took her way back to a specific moment in time. One she remembered quite well.

It was a bright, sunny summer day. Addie and Carrie were little girls still enjoying everything summer had to offer.

"I want a lick of yours," Addie said.

Carrie offered up her red popsicle for Addie to take a lick. "Can I have a lick of yours? I like grape, too."

Addie then pushed her frozen treat in the direction of Carrie's mouth.

The two giggled as they enjoyed the sun and shared licks.

The dresses they wore were the same, except one was

pink and the other was purple. One of the things Addie loved about that dress was the pockets. Their mother often dressed them alike. Addie supposed it was a prerequisite for being sisters born only fifteen months apart.

But that was where the similarities stopped. The sisters couldn't have looked any different. Addie was a brunette with brown eyes and olive skin she inherited from their mother's Italian side of the family. Carrie took after their dad's Swedish roots with blonde hair and bright blue eyes. Carrie's face was fuller than Addie's and always looked as if it glowed. Even as a child, there was something about her that seemed ethereal. More than once over the years, Addie had looked to the top of her sister's head, fully expecting to see a halo. There almost was one in her dream. Or maybe it was an effect of the huge lights that had been blinding her moments ago.

With the popsicles gone, Addie's memories fast-forwarded to a little bit later that same day. From her mind, she watched as she and Carrie twirled in circles, chanting the Ring around the Rosie song. Their dresses flared out wide as they spun around, which was another one of the reasons Addie loved that dress so much. Even in her drug-induced stupor, Addie felt as if she were smiling as she recalled the day. She could almost feel the warm sun on her face and arms.

That afternoon had been so beautiful and warm that Addie brought out her new box of crayons to color in her new coloring book while lying on a blanket in the sun. She had let Carrie use some of her crayons, even though they were special. These were the good crayons; not the ones that Mom usually bought them for school. These were the ones with the sharpener built-in on the back of the box. Addie had bought these with her own money that she had received for her birthday. She had bought a whole pack of paper, too, and she could do whatever she wanted with it. When Addie tried to draw pictures before, Mom had said she was wasting paper, especially when she couldn't get her pictures just right. If they weren't right, she crumpled up one sheet, grabbed another, and started over. But this was a good part of the day.

Then her dreams took a little turn, one for the worse.

Later that same summer day, they were standing in the checkout line at the grocery store with their mom.

"I saw you take that!" Carrie whispered to Addie, who was standing in line beside her.

"Saw me take what?" Addie played dumb at the same time she looked at her mother, who was too preoccupied putting groceries on the counter to pay attention to her daughters' conversation.

"That pack of gum. You need to put it back."

"I didn't take anything."

"I saw you put it in your pocket!"

Turning her back on her sister and walking toward the front of the shopping cart, Addie said, "I don't know what you're talking about."

Carrie just stared at her with a stare that only she could muster, and that stare would become the bane of Addie's existence. Well, one of them. That stare was the one thing Carrie had inherited from their mom.

When Carrie didn't say anything else as Mom put the groceries in the car and they went home, Addie thought the problem was over, but she was wrong. After dinner that evening, her mother came into the girls' bedroom while Addie was alone.

"Is there something you want to tell me?" Mom asked. With her arms akimbo, Addie knew Mom was mad.

Addie played dumb again. She was getting pretty good at that. "About what?"

"I think you know what." Mom stood there staring at Addie, a replay of Carrie's stare at the store.

That was one thing Addie had yet to overcome. That stare. She couldn't stand strong under her mother's stare for very long.

When Addie didn't respond, her mother held out her hand. Addie knew she wanted the gum.

"I don't have it anymore."

"What happened to it?"

"I ate it all."

"Get your shoes on and put your money in your pocket. We're going back to the store to pay for what you stole."

What you stole. Those words would stick with Addie for

a long, long time. Those were the words that changed her relationship with her sister. She couldn't believe it! Carrie had tattled on her. That wasn't what sisters and best friends were supposed to do. It was ridiculous.

Addie's eyes narrowed in anger as she grudgingly did as her mother told her to. When she walked past her father to go out the front door, she noticed he wouldn't even look at her. Anger was seeping from his every pore. Addie could feel it. Twitches on the side of his face told Addie he was gritting his teeth in an effort to maintain control of his emotions. If she were honest, it made her a little bit afraid of her dad. It was in these times of her father's anger that Mom took over. Dad was too enraged to look at her, let alone deal with the issue. A lot of times, Dad would send a look to mom that communicated something between them just before he walked away from whatever situation Addie had caused.

When they arrived at the grocery store, Mom gave Addie instructions. "I'm going to get the manager to come so you can tell him what you did, and then you will apologize and pay for your mistake."

Addie did exactly as her mother told her to, but there was no repentance. She wasn't sorry at all. In fact, that entire incident fueled the animosity Addie held toward Carrie. Sisters were supposed to be there for each other no matter what. Carrie hadn't backed up Addie on this one small thing. What else wouldn't Carrie back her up on? Addie decided she would never be there for Carrie on whatever day she needed it. The whole fiasco gave Addie a desire to make her sister miserable for the rest of her life. A promise Addie had kept since then.

When Mom and Addie got back home, Mom pointed to the blanket and the box of crayons that were still in the yard.

"Go clean up your mess before you come in the house."

Without saying anything, Addie did as she was told. She was afraid if she left her crayons outside at night, something might eat them since the colors were so pretty and had names like peach and cotton candy. They looked yummy enough to eat. When Addie picked up the box, it felt weird. She opened it up to find that all the tips of the crayons had melted into each other. Pulling out the whole thing, Addie hoped she could break them apart and they would be just like new. But they weren't. They weren't easy to break apart, and most of them just broke. Even where the paper was still on the crayons, they were stuck. It didn't take long for Addie to realize her special crayons were ruined. She gathered them up, went into the house, and threw them right into the garbage can. Then she went to her room. It had been such a terrible day she didn't want to be around anybody. Then she realized it was Carrie's fault the crayons were still outside. Addie had come in to get a drink and then Mom had told them to get ready to go to the store. Carrie should have brought them inside with her. It was Carrie's fault that Addie's beautiful crayons were no more.

Addie also recalled this was one of the last days the

sisters were true friends. They had been best friends. They thought nothing could ever separate them or ruin their relationship. Who knew that what would destroy their relationship was Addie herself and a pack of gum? There would be no best of friends. They were the worst of enemies.

∞ ∞ ∞

"Come on, Addie, I need you to wake up."

Someone was gently slapping her face. She didn't want to wake up. She wanted to stay where she was. As she came out of the anesthesia, the memory of the stolen gum sank into the recesses of her brain. Addie felt a little remorse. But then another thought came to her. Did she want to have a relationship with her sister again? She wondered if that statement was true: Could time heal all wounds?

"Addie. Come on. Wake up."

She began to wonder where she was. The pain in her chest came back, too.

"No," was all she said before retreating to a better time and place.

Chapter Two

*A*ddie heard herself groan as she tried to move. There was pain. A lot of pain. When she tried to move, she felt as if something was holding her down. Was something strapped to her face? A whooshing sound seemed to coordinate with the air being forced into her body. Was she on a ventilator? What happened?

That sound made her chest hurt like it was pumping unwanted air into her lungs. She needed to get the thing off her face, but her arms were heavy weights she struggled to raise. There were cords everywhere, including wrapped around her arms. She wondered how she got tangled up in so many cords.

Suddenly, and uninvited, little vignettes of life flashed before her mind. Ethan at the bar. She and Carrie as little girls. Melted crayons?

Voices and a familiar fragrance brought her out of her dreaminess for a moment, but she didn't have the strength to respond to them or even really be able to figure out what the voices were saying. She heard words, but the words didn't make any sense. The only thing she knew for sure was that there were two males in the room.

"Her vitals look great for the circumstances. Heart rate, blood pressure, and pulse are right where we expect them to be at this point."

"Good. You haven't noticed anything alarming?"

"Nothing at all."

"It looks like she might be coming out of it a little bit, but I'd like to keep her under anesthesia a little longer. I want her to remain as still as possible. I want to give the lungs as much opportunity to take as we can. We've never had a better match. Watch for any signs of pneumonia; that's the biggest risk right now. Make sure to check her drainage tubes for anything that doesn't look normal as well, and be sure to check her temperature regularly, too. If it drops, grab one of those blankets from the warmer to cover her with."

"I'll take care of everything."

"I'll check back in a few hours then. If you do notice anything, anything at all, let me know."

"Will do, Doctor."

Addie managed to somewhat turn her head to her left side as she felt someone tugging on her arm. It seemed they tugged a little harder than necessary.

Then came the searing pain that made her flinch.

The nurse must have noticed Addie's half-open eyes as she tried to get something to register. He smiled. Was it a sardonic smile? "You're doing great. I'm giving you some more meds to help you rest."

There was no encouragement or comfort in his tone of voice. Neither was there in the expression on his face.

But then ... Did he look familiar, or was it just Addie's imagination? His closeness brought that smell again. Where did it come from? What was it? Memories seemed just beyond her recall reach. Addie tried to say no, tried to tell the nurse she didn't want any meds. Meds meant more dreams. Her brain digging up old, disturbing memories was not a place she wanted to go. While not scary in themselves, the dreams were unsettling.

Half-conscious, Addie watched as the nurse slipped a needle into her IV. It wasn't long before she was completely unconscious again; the dream world returned, and other memories surfaced.

∞ ∞ ∞

Addie was sitting in the bathroom watching her father shave before church that Sunday morning. She always loved the way he smelled. It was familiar. It smelled of strength and comfort and home. Addie sitting in the bathroom watching him shave was her one special time with Dad each week. It was tradition. She would watch him shave, and he would always put a dot of shaving cream on her nose. She would giggle, and he would smile. It was one of those few moments of peace in Addie's life.

One Sunday morning, before he began his routine, he gave the can a shake. He dropped his hand in feigned frustration. "Remind me to tell your mom to stop using my shaving cream to shave her legs. I guess she wants to smell like a man."

Addie laughed as he squirted out all he could, the manly-smelling foam sputtering and spraying in all directions, which was barely enough to get the job done.

That morning, Carrie came into the bathroom. "I want to watch, too."

"No!" Addie shouted. "This is my time with Daddy. Get out!"

"But I want to watch." Carrie climbed up on the toilet.

"You have your own special Daddy time. This is mine." Instead of waiting for their father to take care of the situation, Addie gave Carrie a shove with her foot.

Screaming, Carrie fell backwards and hit her head on the corner of the cabinet. The sound was a sickening crack.

Addie had never heard Carrie cry so loud. Daddy shot Addie a disappointed look as he picked Carrie up off the floor. That was when Addie noticed all the blood.

"Oh my!" Dad said and placed his hand on Carrie's head, where blood was seeping out of it. "Ellie!" He shouted to get their mother's attention.

"What's all the noise?" she asked as she walked into the bathroom. But then stopped as her question was answered without words. "Oh no! What happened?"

"An accident." Daddy said the word while looking at Addie.

Addie knew he hoped it was an accident, that Addie hadn't meant to hurt her sister. But Addie knew the truth. Addie knew her dad knew the truth. She did mean it. When she shoved Carrie, she didn't know what the outcome would be, but she was pleased with herself. Except maybe for the part where she knew she disappointed her dad. And the blood. There was a lot of blood on the bathroom floor. Carrie really was hurt, Addie thought to herself as she looked at the pool of red liquid that had come out of Carrie's head.

"I'll call your mom to come over and watch Addie." Mommy ran out of the room while Daddy got Carrie into the car. As soon as Grandma arrived, the others left. Addie went right to her room and sobbed into her pillow. She didn't want Grandma to hear her, and she didn't want anyone else to know she felt sorry for her sister. But she did. At least as much as Addie could. But she also felt sorry for herself as Carrie got all the attention.

They didn't go to church that day. Instead, Carrie got her

first stitches. Ten of them.

∞ ∞ ∞

Addie's mind floated from one time period to the next.

This time, her dreams took her to a wedding where Carrie was the flower girl. Addie felt her heart race as anger began to take over. She was so jealous of Carrie in her beautiful dress and made up hair. She even got to wear a little make up that day. Because she was the flower girl, Carrie had spent the day with Aunt Charlotte getting pampered.

Child Addie was jealous. Trying to pull up the memories, adult Addie recalled that Aunt Charlotte had wanted both of them to participate in the wedding, but child Addie was full of attitude.

"I don't want to be in some dumb wedding!"

But when she saw Carrie in the most beautiful dress she had ever seen and her hair done, Addie changed her mind. By the time Addie realized she did want to be in the wedding, it was too late.

Meekly, she went up to Aunt Charlotte in the bride's room, where Addie's mom was helping Carrie get ready. "I want to be in the wedding now."

Mom had heard and spoke up. "It's too late, honey. If you wanted to be in the wedding, you needed to tell us months ago."

Aunt Charlotte knelt in front of Addie. "I'm so sorry, sweetie. Do you want to help and do another job?"

Addie didn't want to do anything except be dressed up as beautiful as Carrie, but she found herself nodding her head anyway.

Aunt Charlotte smiled. "Do you want to welcome people and show them where to sign the guest book?"

She didn't, but apparently, she had no choice in the matter. One of the other girls in the room, who wasn't in the wedding either, took Addie by the hand and led her to the foyer of the church where the guest book was located. She and Addie stood together, but Addie never said a word to anyone that came through the doors. The other girl was doing all the talking, not that Addie wanted to or anything.

What made it even worse was that Carrie was in all the pictures. Six-year-old Addie sat with her arms crossed in front of her, eyes once again narrowed toward her sister. She fumed inwardly as she waited for her parents. Then something dawned on her. Aunt Charlotte wanted Carrie in the wedding because she was blonde. Aunt Charlotte had blonde hair and blue eyes, just like Carrie, while Addie had brown hair and eyes. Not to mention that Carrie's hair could be styled beautifully. Addie's curly hair, on the other hand, was unruly, much like she was and could never be tamed into submission for very long. That made Addie even madder. It also made her dislike of her sister grow even *deeper. She didn't think "hate" because that was a word her mom wouldn't allow her to say. But she was close to saying it because she sure did feel it.*

Other pictures flashed through Addie's memories as she drifted in and out of a semi-conscious state. As she grew older in her mind, she saw herself as the bad sister and Carrie as the good one. In all the movies she had ever seen, the princess was always blonde, and the bad witch was always a brunette. Irony at its best.

In her half-comatose state, Addie thought about how it seemed everyone had always been against her for some reason. That had stuck with her all her life. Snippets of offenses from other people popped in and out of her mind.

Then she noticed that same smell again. The good one that stood out above all the antiseptic smells of the hospital. Addie willed her eyes to open, but it was as if they were stuck shut. She couldn't even raise her hands to pry her lids upward. Then she felt herself dozing off again, too tired to even think about the fragrance that enveloped her. Sleep claimed her before she realized she was not alone.

∞ ∞ ∞

Carrie's first day of kindergarten burst into Addie's dreams. She thought it was funny she could remember Carrie's first day of school but not her own. Addie spent her kindergarten year getting into trouble and even being kicked out of school for a week. Who had ever been kicked out of kindergarten? Addie was proud of her status as the bad kid. It forced Mom and Dad to look at and notice her.

On Carrie's first day of school, she did everything little kids do in excited anticipation of meeting new friends. After some school shopping, she picked an outfit and packed her bag with all her brand new school supplies.

"Do you think they'll like me, Mommy?"

"Of course they will, sweetheart!"

"But what if I don't make any friends?"

"Why wouldn't you make any friends? You already know a lot of your classmates."

Carrie shrugged her shoulders and put her head down. Addie could tell she was a little scared, but she didn't try to encourage her sister at all.

Mom got down on her knees in front of Carrie and took her by the shoulders. "Instead of worrying about who is going to make friends with you, why don't you take the first steps? If you see a classmate who looks a bit frightened, go and talk to them and try to make them feel better.

Kindergarten can be a scary thing, especially on the first day."

Taking a deep breath, Carrie gave one emphatic nod of her head. "I'll make sure everyone has a friend and that no one is being mean or picking on someone else."

"Good girl."

Always the good girl.

The girls happened to have recess at the same time that school year. Addie usually hogged a swing while she watched Carrie run around to all her classmates and made sure they were having fun. Everyone loved Carrie. She made everyone smile as soon as they saw her. Students waved as she walked past them. Even teachers waved and smiled in her direction.

Addie knew no one felt the same about her, and she was tired of it. About halfway through the school year, she wanted to teach Carrie a lesson. And Addie saw her moment. A small boy was hiding in a corner the outer walls of the school building made. From her perch on the swing, Addie could see his clothes weren't as nice as hers. With the way he was sitting and his pants hiked up some, she could also see that his socks didn't match. And it wasn't the purposeful mismatch some of the kids did. Formulating a plan in her head, Addie jumped off the swing and slowly headed in his direction. She didn't want anyone to see her, and she knew her teacher watched her carefully. Addie was sure her kindergarten teacher had told the first grade teacher of all the things she had done the previous year. When Addie walked into her first grade classroom at the beginning of the year, she could tell the teacher already didn't like her, especially since her desk was at the front of the room, right in front of the teacher's.

Out of the corner of her eye, she saw her teacher watching her. Addie bent down to the ground, acting as if she was looking at something in the dirt. When her teacher looked away to speak to another adult, Addie made her move. She walked over to stand next to where the boy slouched down against the wall of the school.

"What are you doing?" she asked.

"Nothing."

"Why don't you go out there and play?"

"I don't want to."

"Why? Because you smell bad, and the other kids make fun of you?"

He didn't answer. He just pulled his knees up closer to his face and wrapped his arm around his shins as if to protect himself.

"Or is it because your parents don't give you nice clothes? Your socks have holes in them."

Addie wasn't sure, but she thought she heard a sniffle coming from his direction. A devious smile slowly spread across her lips. "Do they even send you to school with food for lunch?"

She had more mean things to say, but they were abruptly

cut off when someone shoved her from behind. When she turned around, she saw Carrie.

"You're not being kind!" shouted her sister.

"How would you know? You weren't over here?"

"I heard you be mean to him."

By this time, the teachers had come over to see what the problem was, which Carrie felt obliged to share. "Addie was being mean to Colin."

"Let's go inside, Addie. I think you've had enough playground time today." Her teacher forcefully grabbed her by the hand and practically dragged her into the school building.

As Addie struggled to keep up with her teacher, she was able to turn around and see Carrie kneeling beside Colin talking to him. She took his hand and pulled him to a standing position before they walked off together to some other part of the playground.

When the girls got home that afternoon, Carrie was in tears.

"Carrie, what's the matter?" Mom asked.

"My crayons!" was all she could blubber out.

Addie stood there looking as innocent as she possibly could.

"What's the matter with your crayons?"

"They're all broken!"

Mom pulled the box of crayons out of Carrie's bag and inspected them. They were, in fact, all broken. With a not quite accusatory glance at Addie, she said, "I wonder how that happened. I'll have Daddy stop and pick another box up on his way home from work tonight. Okay?"

All Carrie could do was nod. As she wiped tears and snot off her face with the back of her hand, Mom had an idea.

"We can melt these and make some fun crayons for you to keep at home. How would you like that?"

Again, Carrie nodded her head and sniffed.

"Why don't you go wash your hands and face while I get some things out and ready in the kitchen? But then I'll need your help. We have to take off all the paper wrappings."

As Carrie bounced away to obey, Mom looked questioningly at Addie. She didn't even have to say a word. She knew, but Addie wasn't going to let that make a difference in her response.

"It wasn't me. We aren't even in the same classroom."

Mom must have heard Carrie opening the bathroom door to come out, so she didn't say anything else.

By the time Carrie came into the kitchen, she was her normal self again. Happy-go-lucky. She hopped up on one of the bar stools at the counter where Mom had placed the crayons and a couple of bowls.

"Peel the paper off the crayons and then put the paper in this bowl and put the crayon pieces in this bowl," Mom gave simple instructions. "Do you want to help us, Addie? You guys can share the crayons."

"Nope." Addie didn't want to have anything to do with it.

She already played with those crayons enough last night after Carrie had gone to bed.

After that day, Addie watched as Carrie befriended everyone. No one was left standing alone. If a student didn't have to be picked last for a team, Carrie would have changed that, too. But someone had to inevitably be chosen last.

Carrie would always be first.

Addie would always be last.

Chapter Three

*P*ain. The pain in her chest was so great Addie felt as if she was dying. She tried to move, but it still seemed as if she was strapped to the bed with all the cords keeping her attached to it.

Cold. Suddenly, she noticed the cold. She was colder than she had ever been. Was she outside? Was it winter? It was dark, that was for sure. Maybe?

But were her eyes open or closed? She couldn't tell.

Addie thought she heard a voice in the distance. It was so far away Addie wasn't sure if it was talking to her or about her or someone else entirely. Or maybe there wasn't anyone there at all but her mind playing tricks on her.

"Let's keep her in a coma. I don't want her moving around. Also, her temp seems to be a little low. Grab me one of those heated blankets."

Soon, Addie felt an unexpected weight and warmth overtake her. Blissfully, she fell back into a deep sleep.

Away from the cold. Away from the cords. Away from the hissing and beeping of medical machinery and excruciating pain.

But not away from the nightmares that plagued her. She wasn't sure which was worse.

∞   ∞   ∞

"Snow day!" Carrie ran around the house shouting. As usual, her smile and laughter were infectious. Except to Addie.

Perfect, *Addie smiled to herself. She hadn't completed the mammal project that was due today anyway. Mrs. Williams had told Addie if she was late with this project, she would receive a failing grade. It wasn't the first time Addie was late with a school project. She didn't care. It wouldn't be the last time, either.*

It wasn't very often they got a day off from school because of snow, but during the night more than fifteen inches had fallen. The temperature was below zero, and Addie decided it was a good day to spend in bed.

But Mom wasn't having any of that.

"I think we're going to take the opportunity to do a thorough cleaning of the house. I'll make up a list of chores, and you can each pick three off it. When you finish your list, the rest of the day is yours to do as you please."

"I'm going to do mine right now."

"Without a doubt." Addie couldn't help but respond to Carrie's overt happiness. Did she ever stop smiling or, as she called it, looking on the bright side? It was annoying.

"But if we hurry, we can get everything done and then go play out in the snow."

"I don't know," Mom spoke up before Addie had a chance to come up with a witty but nasty retort to Carrie. "It's awfully cold outside."

"We don't have to stay out long." Carrie tried to convince Mom. "Besides, we have those hats, gloves, and scarves Grandma Hazel knitted for us. Those are the warmest things ever!"

Addie did have to agree with that. Last Christmas, Grandma Hazel had gifted them the outer wear. They were so warm, but as usual, Addie's gift was less than. While Carrie got a set in her favorite color, Addie's set was black. Boring, old, ugly black. When Addie had commented on it then, Grandma had only said she didn't know what Addie's favorite color was. Well, she knew Carrie's favorite color! Would it have killed her to ask someone? Anyone? Addie chalked it up to the fact that Grandma just didn't care enough about her to take the extra effort. Grandma Hazel was definitely not Grandma Marjie. She wished it had been Grandma Hazel that died, not Grandma Marjie.

As usual, Carrie flew through her chores. That left Addie to clean the upstairs bathroom she and Carrie shared, vacuum the rug in the living room after moving the furniture, and clean the outsides of the kitchen cabinets. When Carrie was done, she found Addie parked on the couch in front of the TV.

"Are you done already? I took the chores that would take longest so you wouldn't have to work so hard, and we could go out and play."

Addie rolled her eyes. She couldn't believe what she just heard. It was all a lie.

"I didn't do my chores yet, but I don't want to go out."

"Come on! Sledding and building snow forts is so much more fun when we do it together. You're better at making the sledding paths than I am."

There was that. Addie's snow forts were way better than Carrie's. And when Addie formed a sledding path through the deep snow, she added ramps covered in ice that would send the girls flying.

"I'll be out in a while." Addie really had no intention of going outside, but she figured the conversation wouldn't go away until she said something appeasing.

"Hurry up! I'll go get started!"

And off Carrie ran in a flurry to get outside.

Who wanted to be outside when it was ten degrees below zero?

About an hour later, Mom called Carrie inside.

"I'm waiting for Addie."

"You're going to be waiting a long time. She hasn't left

the couch yet."

Addie again rolled her eyes. She hated it when people talked about her like she couldn't hear them. She was right here! She could hear everything Mom said.

"I want you to come in and warm up. I've made you some hot cocoa."

In seconds, Addie heard Carrie come through the door. As she dropped her boots and snowsuit at the door, she filled Addie in on all the details she never cared to know.

"I started on a sledding path, but it's not as good as yours. I can't make the jumps like you can. Then I started on a snow fort at the end of the driveway where Dad and the snowplow piled up all the snow. The snowplow left some ginormous snow clumps that were perfect for the base."

She rambled on. Addie turned up the volume of the TV to try and drown out her sister's voice. Then Mom came in and turned the TV off.

Smiling at Addie, she said, "It's lunch time. You've watched enough television today. After you eat, you'll do your chores."

Yes, Mom was smiling, but it was a sinister smile. Addie could never understand why her supposed family insisted on making her life miserable.

Again, Addie was awake. More or less. She felt groggier than she had ever felt in her life. She also felt as if there was an elephant sitting on her chest. At least the whooshing sound and whatever had covered her face seemed to be gone. Voices made noise around her, but she couldn't make sense of them.

"She's not coming out of it like she should be."

"What does that mean?"

"In a word, it means I'm worried about her. We should have her up and walking by now."

"Do you think she'll be okay?"

"Honestly, in all the years I've been a doctor, I have never seen anything like this."

Sniffles sounded near Addie's ear.

"Can I be open with you?"

"Absolutely."

"I can't help but wonder if there is something that is keeping her out of it. Her blood pressure and heart rate are fine when she's 'awake' but skyrocket when she's asleep. That's not normal. That tells me it might be something psychological. Maybe she's reliving the nightmare. We have been giving her pain medication since pulling her out of the coma, but it shouldn't knock her out like this. I've seen this in accident patients before. Many don't want to face the reality that awaits them. There's something in their subconscious at work. I don't understand it because

I'm not that kind of a doctor. I have just seen it before. And knowing what I know about this particular accident—"

"What can we do?"

"All I can suggest is that you stay near her. Hold her hand. Speak to her. Try to give her comfort in every way. There is some reason she doesn't want to wake up. Maybe she feels guilty about something in her life."

Were they talking about her?

Some of the voices sounded familiar. Maybe? Maybe not? Nothing seemed certain. Voices were calling her name. She felt something tugging on her arm, but it felt strange, as if she weren't really connected to her body.

"Come on, Adeline, we need you here with us."

Addie wanted to stay where the voices were, but something deeper called to her. Her dreams.

It was Daddy/daughter date time. Seven-year-old Addie looked at herself in the full-length mirror and twirled, her dress billowing out around her. Tonight was the night she and Daddy got to spend together. Just the two of them with no Carrie. Daddy always made these nights special. Mom

had helped Addie get dressed and do her hair. She even put the tiniest bit of make-up on Addie's cheeks. These were always good days, days Addie looked forward to.

Tonight, they were going to Addie's favorite restaurant for dinner, then to the movies, and finally to get ice cream for dessert. Addie was excited that she was going to be out late. Since she didn't have to get up for school in the morning, so it was okay.

The night was perfect. Almost. At least until Mom called in the middle of the movie.

Dad suddenly grabbed Addie's hand and pulled her from the theater so he wouldn't disturb those who were still watching the movie.

"What? Are you sure?" he asked when they had exited the theater.

Addie could hear her mom's panicked voice coming through the phone.

"Yes! I'm sure. Please come home right now. We need to get her to the doctor."

That was it. Addie's special night with Dad was over. Carrie needed him more. After swallowing a nickel earlier in the day, Carrie was now crying because of stomach pain. Mom wanted to take her to the emergency room. That was where Addie found herself. Sitting in the waiting room in her beautiful dress, waiting. Waiting for Dad to come and take her back out to finish their evening. Waiting for Carrie to get rid of the nickel. Addie had overheard how the doctor *said it would come out and found it disgusting. A nurse gave Carrie something to drink that was supposed to help speed the process along a little faster. Addie wasn't exactly sure what that meant, except that she was out here in the waiting room, by herself, under the watchful eye of the nurse at the desk who happened to be their next-door neighbor. That was just one of the perks of small-town living – everyone knew everyone else.*

It was late when all was said and done. Dad held Carrie in his arms as Mom tried to shake Addie awake. "Come on, Addie. It's time to go home."

Addie could barely open her eyes enough to walk to the car. Mom did hold her hand, but Addie wished she was being carried as well.

That was the end of their Daddy/daughter date.

Later, in a brief moment of clarity, Addie remembered other Daddy/daughter dates through the years. She knew her Dad tried to make them enjoyable, but the older she got, the more difficult it was. There were some days she felt her father only took her out because he was doing penance for some great sin he had committed when he was younger. What that was, Addie didn't know. What she did know for sure was that even her dad didn't seem to like taking her out. Maybe Mom made him do it, or maybe he did it out of obligation because she was his daughter. Whatever the reason, both parties wished they could be anywhere else but together.

Chapter Four

"I don't understand. What's the matter with her?"

Addie was fairly certain it was her mother's voice she heard from the depths of wherever she was. Mom's was the first voice she could actually name for certain, even though others sounded familiar.

"Her body might be rejecting the lungs. We've put her on an immunosuppressant to help with that."

"Why is she rejecting them? I thought they were a perfect match."

"It is a perfect match. I don't have answers as to why she might be rejecting it. It could be any number of reasons. Maybe there's the beginning of an infection. Often after a major surgery, the body's immunity is low. The body is an amazing thing. Even with all our knowledge, we still don't understand all its capabilities."

"Is there a chance they will take?"

"Yes. I still can't help but think there is something else going on here as well. The mind has a lot to do with a person's health. I told you before that I feel Addie's been struggling this entire time, and I wonder if there is something psychological going on that we can't see. We obviously can't talk to her about it or bring in a psychologist until she is fully awake and coherent."

Addie heard what she thought were sniffles and then the sound of a zipper being forcefully pulled. While Addie couldn't open her eyes or even move, she could imagine her mom searching through her purse for a tissue.

"Here." That was the male voice again.

Swoosh came the sound of a tissue being pulled out of a box. Addie was cognizant enough to realize her hearing was amazing. She recalled a health class in school when she was truly listening where her teacher said blind people's senses are often stronger because they depend on them more to "see" what is going on around them. Was that happening now?

"I just don't understand what's going on with her! You assured me this would work!" Her mother could barely squeak out the words.

The sound of a chair scraping across the floor filled Addie's ears.

When the man spoke again, it was from a different

position than before, as if he had sat down in front of Addie's mom to try and give comfort.

"I don't understand everything either. With this type of surgery, there are no guarantees. I've been a doctor for more than twenty years and have never seen a case like this before. That's why I mentioned the mental issues."

Mental issues! Does he think I have mental issues? Addie was screaming in her head, but she couldn't make anything come out of her mouth.

"I really think there is something psychological going on. Maybe she doesn't want to live. Maybe you or your husband can shed some light on her mental state before the accident."

Mom sighed. "I don't even know where to begin there."

What? Addie wanted to shout again. If she did have psychological issues, it was because of her family and the way they treated her.

"Is there some reason she might not want to continue living?"

"I really don't know the answer to that. She's always been ... difficult but never suicidal."

"All we can do is keep a close eye on her and hope we see some improvement soon. Maybe later we could look into some counseling."

Mom snorted at that. "She was never up for it

before."

"Well, a lot has changed."

"Isn't that the truth!"

Addie could imagine her mom shaking her head, desperate for answers. Crying. Mopping up tears that wouldn't stop coming.

In some ways, Addie felt sorry for her, but in other ways, Addie felt her mom deserved everything she was feeling. Carrie was always the favorite. Mom needed to just go take care of her.

∞ ∞ ∞

"It's not my mess!"

"Well, it isn't mine, either."

"It is, too! You need to pick that up!"

"I saw you with it the other day."

"I was throwing it to your side of the room!"

"What is all the commotion in here?" Mom came in when the shouting had escalated to an unreasonable decibel.

"I'm trying to clean, but Addie isn't helping."

"I am, too! You just think all the mess is mine."

This was not a new argument. It was one the sisters had fairly regularly.

"I wish I could put you in different rooms. Then we would see who the mess really belongs to."

"Me too!" The girls said in unison while giving each other a nasty look.

Addie could tell Mom was frustrated. She was usually the mediator between them. "I'm a little tired of being the referee. I'll be right back." Mom left the room. "Keep working," she hollered as she walked down the stairs.

Carrie went back to putting her laundry away. Addie went back to pushing things around. She hated cleaning their bedroom. It was always a mess, and she didn't care. She wondered why her mom and Carrie were so adamant about keeping it clean.

It wasn't too long before Mom came back armed with colored tape. "We are going to split this room in half. You will each be responsible for your half. You will keep your belongings in your half."

Addie and Carrie watched as Mom went about putting lines of tape throughout the room. One went down the center after she kicked all the junk out of the way. Stuff went flying everywhere because Mom was on a mission. In less than thirty minutes, the room was completely divided in half. The pink side was Carrie's, and the purple side was Addie's. The closet was divided from ceiling to floor. Furniture was rearranged to make the room more accessible now that the space was apportioned equally.

The room was also more of a mess than it had been before.

"Now, if you want to eat dinner tonight, I suggest you get

busy. No clean room, no dinner." With that, Mom left them to their work.

Addie stared Carrie down. "This is all your fault."

Carrie sighed. "Let's just clean up." Carrie got busy. When she found something on her side that was Addie's, she laid it on Addie's bed.

Addie wasn't really picking anything up, except when she saw something that was Carrie's. She picked it up and threw it to the opposite side of the room with no care for where it landed. She could tell it was making Carrie mad, so she did it even more. With Mom throwing everything around, a good portion of Carrie's stuff had landed on Addie's side of the room. And vice versa.

After an hour, Addie noticed Carrie was making good progress. Her side was almost completely clean. Addie's side looked like it had hardly been touched.

"How are we doing in here?" Mom's voice drew the attention of both girls.

"I'm almost done."

Naturally, Carrie was almost done. She was the obedient one. She was the one who always did the right thing.

"Good job! I appreciate it." Mom looked at Addie's side. She made a face that told Addie she wasn't pleased with her progress, or lack thereof. "Plan on eating dinner tonight?"

Her tone of voice angered Addie. "I'm not hungry anyway."

Mom shrugged her shoulders. "Too bad. We're going out

for pizza."

One of Addie's favorites.

Mom smiled then. "You still have time before Dad gets home. If you concentrate on working, I'm sure you can be done in time."

"Done!" Carrie spoke up from her side of the room.

Under her breath, Addie mocked her sister.

"I found that book I started reading last month. I think I'm going to go sit out on the porch and read until Dad comes home."

After Carrie and Mom left the room, Addie slumped down on her bed. It would take several more hours to clean up her side. A night out for pizza was out of the question for her. Then her mind went wild. Mom must have planned that on purpose. Mom knew Carrie would obey. She knew Addie had a whole lot more to clean up than Carrie did. Mom just wanted to take Carrie out for dinner and not her.

"Carrie's always the favorite," Addie mumbled as she gave a pile of laundry a kick.

She thought back to a time when they were learning the Ten Commandments in Sunday school. As usual, Carrie was the first one to come to church with the list firmly secured in her head. She spouted off the list of rules they needed to follow. Addie never memorized them completely. Ever since Carrie had memorized them, she followed them to a T and reminded Addie of them whenever she got the chance. So, what was the purpose in Addie memorizing them?

Why did Carrie have to be so ... good?

∞ ∞ ∞

Too soon, or not soon enough, the voices called her back from the dreams.

"Addie! Addie! Can you hear me?"

"She's still not responding!"

Addie felt the slaps on her face but couldn't do anything about them besides let it happen.

"Why isn't she coming out of it?"

"Is she allergic to anything? Check her charts."

There was a rustling of papers.

"No allergies."

"How is her breathing?"

"Right where expected."

"Heart rate?"

"Good."

"Maybe she just needs a little more time."

"It's already been two weeks."

"Don't leave her side."

"I won't."

"Let me know of any changes immediately."

"I will."

None of the voices were familiar. Together, they formed a cacophony of sound that didn't make any sense to her. What were they talking about? Was something wrong with her? Was she stuck in some strange dreamland?

Ahhh! Dreamland. That was where she wanted to be, and for the moment, that was where she was going to stay.

∞ ∞ ∞

Back in her dreams once again, Addie found herself in a place she would rather not be, whether in her dreams or not. Church. It was yet another day Addie's mind recalled without much thought. It was their first day at a new church. Mom and Dad had decided their old church was too far to drive to anymore.

"It's just too hard to get everyone ready to leave so early," Mom had said.

Addie read between those lines. "Addie, you're too difficult to get out of bed and get presentable looking. We're tired of the fighting every Sunday morning, so we're making a change whether you like it or not."

Addie didn't like it. She didn't like it before they left the house, and she didn't like it as soon as they arrived.

The church building was old. It was an old country church that looked like it could have been on the set of Little House on the Prairie.

"We'll come pick you up after Sunday school is over so you

can sit in church with us."

"Dad, we aren't babies!" Addie had copped the attitude of a teenager, even though she was only ten years old.

"It's just that it's a new place, and we don't want you to get lost."

Addie rolled her eyes. "How can we get lost when there are only three rooms in the whole building?"

"We'll come get you after Sunday school." Dad's voice was firm, and he and Mom turned and left the room before Addie could argue more.

Addie didn't miss the cringing smile her mom gave to the new teacher, Miss Judy.

"Why don't you girls sit right over here?" Miss Judy pulled out a couple of chairs. "I have a treat for you."

Addie knew it wouldn't take long for Miss Judy's smile to get on her nerves.

"There's a little game my brother and I used to play when we were kids. There were times he would be mean when we were playing this game, but I promise to be nice. So, here goes, open your mouth and close your eyes, and I will give you a big surprise."

Addie sneered at Carrie, who was all for the game. Carrie was rewarded with popping candy. Addie could hear it snapping in Carrie's mouth. When Miss Judy held up the envelope for Addie to receive some, Addie shook her head.

"I don't want any."

Addie had to watch in disgust as Miss Judy went around the table to give each of the students their prize. Did she think they were babies? Why couldn't they each have their own envelope of candy? Addie wasn't much into sharing with anyone, particularly with strangers.

The rest of the class did not improve.

"Have you children ever heard the story of Jacob and Esau?"

Immediately, Carrie's hand flew up in the air, bumping Addie in the process. "I have! They were twins."

Miss Judy's eyes got huge, like she was surprised that anyone would have heard of Jacob and Esau. One didn't have to spend too much time in a church building before hearing about Jacob and Esau.

"Yes, they were twins. They were the only children born to Isaac and Rebekah. For those who have been attending class, you'll remember that Isaac was the promised son of Abraham and Sarah.

"When mommies are expecting a baby, their bellies get big, and you can feel the baby moving around. Well, Rachel could certainly feel her babies moving. It felt as if they were fighting or having a wrestling match."

Miss Judy picked up her Bible and read a verse. "'And the LORD said unto her, Two nations are in thy womb, and two manner of people shall be separated from thy bowels; and the one people shall be stronger than the other people; and the elder shall serve the younger.'

"Remember that it was the firstborn son who would receive the birthright and be highly favored and blessed by the father. Esau was born first, followed by his brother, Jacob.

"Many years later, Jacob had cooked some food while

Esau had been out hunting. When Esau came home, he was almost starving; at least that's what he said. He begged Jacob for some of the delicious smelling food. Jacob would give it to him, but it would come at a price. Esau had to sell his birthright for a simple bowl of stew."

Addie was doing all she could to stay awake. She had heard this story many times and never once liked it.

"Jacob was a sneaky brother. When it came time for his father to bless his oldest son, Jacob and Rebekah tricked him. Jacob ended up receiving the birthright blessing instead of Esau."

She paused for a moment and looked around the table. "Have you ever taken anything that didn't belong to you? Maybe something that belonged to one of your brothers or sisters?"

Addie did not intend to answer that question out loud.

Several of the other children did raise their hands, including Carrie. Addie realized she was the only one who hadn't raised her hand. She didn't care.

"After this all happened," Miss Judy continued with the story, "Esau was mad, as he had every right to be, and Jacob had to leave home and go far away where his brother couldn't hurt him."

Miss Judy then put on a very serious face. "Who wants to be like Jacob in the story? A deceiver and a liar?"

"Not me," came from several seats around the table.

"No," Miss Judy agreed. "We want to treat others with kindness and fairness every day."

Addie escaped into her thoughts. She didn't want to hear

any more of what Miss Judy had to say. Addie knew she was much more like Jacob than she was Esau. That was the way she wanted it. Jacob was strong for standing up for what was his. If Esau wanted to give up something so important so easily, that was his problem. Jacob bought the birthright fair and square.

Rousing a little bit, Addie awoke with Jacob and Esau still on her mind. She always felt a little bit like Esau; she was the true firstborn in her family, but it seemed Carrie got all the praise and the blessings. Carrie stole Addie's birthright and became the favored one. Addie then recalled that the following week, Miss Judy had told the story of Cain and Abel. That was another Bible story Carrie knew every detail of. Addie knew it as well; she just wasn't about to let anyone know she knew it. Abel was the perfect, obedient brother who did everything he was told to the letter. He brought a blood sacrifice to worship God. Addie always held a soft spot in her heart—if there was one—for Abel. She always felt he had done his best and brought God the best of his crops. Sure, God had made a point of telling them their sacrifices needed to be a blood offering, but Abel didn't have any sheep. What was he supposed to do?

Another fact Addie knew was that she had been the bad sister. Everyone else knew it, too.

It wasn't long after they started attending the new church that Addie found out what her mother had done. Before dropping them off in the children's Sunday school class, she had called Miss Judy and told her about Addie's attitude. When Addie found out, it made her attitude even worse. Why couldn't her parents leave well enough alone? Why couldn't they let people make their own opinions of Addie as they got to know her instead of tainting those opinions even before meeting her?

Life just wasn't fair. It wasn't fair for Jacob or Abel, and it wasn't fair for Addie.

Chapter Five

*A*ddie was struggling to become conscious. She knew there was something close at hand that she was trying to figure out, but her mind couldn't wrap around the thought long enough to grab hold of it.

"You deserve this."

It was a somewhat familiar voice. It was male, but it wasn't her father. Addie then heard moaning. It seemed to be coming from her own body.

"It should have been you."

Then she felt a sharp stabbing pain, which made her moan louder. If only the fuzziness in her mind would clear, maybe she could figure things out.

"The only reason I'm giving you any medication at all is because I have to; I don't want to lose my job. You deserve every bit of pain you're feeling. I wish I could make you feel more. For the rest of your life."

Where was she?

What had happened to her?

Who was speaking?

It seemed to be only mere seconds before the fuzziness took complete control, and Addie once again knew nothing of what was going on around her. There were only her dreams.

Run! *Addie told herself. It hurt to breathe, but she felt the need to run. Everything around her was dark. The streets were dark. The buildings were dark. It must have rained because her bare feet repeatedly splashed down in puddles, soaking the hem of her nightgown. Every once in a while, a light would shine on the puddles, but Addie couldn't tell where the light came from. With repeated looks back, she could see, in spite of the darkness, the shadow of what looked like a man coming after her. She could not see his face, but it frightened her. There was no time to stop and catch her breath even though her lungs burned. She wasn't sure what the man wanted or why he was following her, but she could not stop to find out. She stopped and banged on unlocked doors only to receive no answer and stumble to the next.*

Shadows were all around her; she sensed them reaching out to her, trying to grab her. Addie dodged one shadow after another. In her dream, she screamed when something caught hold of her nightgown and pulled on it.

"No!" Addie tugged her clothing back and wrapped it around her tightly so it was out of reach of the shadows.

"Come!" The voice called out to her again and again.

She knew it was the man calling her, but she feared stopping. What if it was a trick? A scam? A way to subdue her? No. She couldn't and wouldn't stop running, no matter how much it hurt to breathe.

As she opened her eyes, a form at the door caught her attention.

"Dad?" Her voice was barely a whisper, and she wasn't even sure it had been her father. Maybe she only wanted it to be him for the safety he could offer from her nightmares.

∞ ∞ ∞

A familiar voice started to bring Addie out of her drug-induced stupor.

"Honey, it's Mom. Can you hear me?"

Addie responded by slightly moving her head back and forth. In her mind, she wanted to fully open her eyes and speak to her mom. She wanted to know where she was and what she was doing there. Why was she in so much pain? She wanted to escape her nightmares.

Suddenly, she felt a squeeze on her right hand. Was that her mom? Addie tried with all the strength she had in her to give her mom, or whoever it was, a squeeze back to let them know she was here.

Her hand fell to the bad as soon as Addie thought she sent that squeeze.

"Nurse! I think she's coming out of it. She squeezed my hand!"

Some sort of pounding sent her head reeling. Whatever that noise was, it needed to stop. When someone started patting her cheek, she figured the pounding was the noise of a nurse's steps entering the room. But they sure were loud.

"Adeline, can you hear me?"

That definitely wasn't Mom. Mom rarely called her Adeline. Only when she was in trouble. Which was actually a lot.

Their names were ridiculous. Addie had that thought every time she had to write out her full name. Many times people would comment on it, especially the old ladies.

"What a sweet, old-fashioned name!" they would squeak out in their old lady voices. "I used to have a friend with that same name when I was a little girl."

That was the whole reason Addie hated her name. She wasn't born an old lady. Her parents shouldn't have given her an old lady name. But as the story went, her mother had found the names while doing some genealogical research on her family history when she was in high school. Somewhere back in the pages of time, they had ancestor twin sisters by the names of Adeline and Caroline. Her mom had vowed to name her girls after them if she ever had daughters. And it was a story she didn't mind sharing. Every time she introduced her daughters to anyone new.

"Aren't they the cutest names you've ever heard? When I discovered the names of twins in my family history, I knew I needed to remember them for later. And look! God blessed me with two daughters so I could use the names. It just goes to show how much God loves us when He gives us even the smallest desires of our hearts!"

That was Mom. Always sharing how God was at work in her life. It never ceased to annoy Addie if she was anywhere nearby. As she got older, she learned the cue words and would escape to a different aisle of the store, if possible, until her mom finished talking and telling her ridiculous story.

At least Addie didn't have to keep going by Adeline. Addie sounded a little better. However, she had considered legally changing her name completely multiple times.

"Addie, I need to know if you can hear me. Can you nod your head?"

Addie tried, but moving her head was difficult and

extremely painful.

"Can you squeeze my hand?"

Addie felt a hand come into her own. Squeeze a hand. She could do that. At least, she thought she could.

A cheerful "Good job!" was the reward for her successful squeeze. It wasn't her mom's voice, so it must have still been the nurse.

Addie was exhausted after all the excitement. Again, she heard voices around her, but they didn't make much sense.

"I think she's going to be just fine. I'll make sure to put a note in her chart so the doctor can see it when he comes in. It will make him happy to see at least a little bit of a response from her."

"Thank you so much!"

"Mom?" It was barely a whisper, but Addie felt someone sit on the edge of the bed.

"I'm here, sweetheart. I'm here."

Addie surprisingly found comfort in that. As she slipped into a deep but restless sleep, she hoped her mom would still be holding her hand when she awoke.

Mrs. Greene. That name had not come to her mind for

years. Addie wondered what made it come to the surface now in her dreams.

"Are you girls ready?" Mrs. Greene asked as she walked right into the house without even knocking.

For some reason, that annoyed Addie.

"I am!" Carrie came bouncing into the room.

"Do you have your Bible, Addie?" Mom asked.

Rolling her eyes, Addie turned around and stomped off to her room to get the Bible.

Mrs. Greene was one of those ladies Addie always thought stuck her nose in other people's business. She often offered to take the girls to church events when both their parents were working. Addie had been looking forward to getting out of going to Vacation Bible School this week. Who wanted to spend every single day at church for a whole week over the summer? Addie was elated when mom's car had some mechanical issues and had to be in the shop the entire week of Vacation Bible School.

"I'll pick them up and bring them home," Addie had overheard Mrs. Greene telling her mom on Sunday at church. "I have to be there to teach anyway, and I have to drive right by your house."

"That sounds wonderful! I would hate for them to miss it as it is their favorite week of the summer."

Maybe Carrie's, but not mine, Addie grumbled in her head.

Every morning that week, Mrs. Greene picked up Carrie

and Addie. On the first day, Carrie tried to sit up front. That would've been okay with Addie. That would keep the conversation between the two of them in the front. However, Mrs. Greene said, "Everyone in the back. I feel safer with my passengers in the back seat." Addie was at least grateful for the equal footing when it seemed everyone else catered to Carrie and all her wants and demands.

Each day, as they got in the car to drive home, Mrs. Greene asked them what they learned. Carrie was always right there with an answer.

"Our verse for today was Ephesians 4:32. 'And be ye kind, one to another, tenderhearted forgiving one another, even as God for Christ's sake hath forgiven you.'"

"Wow! You memorized it already!" Mrs. Greene was impressed.

Carrie shrugged her shoulders. "I learned it a long time ago."

"Well," Mrs. Greene started, "did you learn anything new?"

It only took Carrie a moment to think. "Yes! Kindness is one of the fruits of the Spirit. When we show kindness, we are living as Jesus lived. I can't wait to learn about the rest of the fruits this week."

Addie just rolled her eyes.

"What about you, Addie? Did you learn something new today?"

"Basically what Carrie already said, but I don't have the

verse memorized yet." She hoped that was enough for Mrs. Greene to put her attention back on Carrie, who actually wanted to talk about what she had learned.

Nope.

"Well, what was your favorite part of the day then?" Mrs. Green wouldn't let Addie get away without saying something.

Addie wracked her brain, trying to come up with something acceptable.

Snack time?

No.

Game time.

No.

Time to go home?

No.

Song time?

Maybe.

"Singing all the fun songs."

Addie may have fooled Mrs. Greene, but there was no fooling Carrie, who sat in her corner of the back seat with her arms crossed tight over her chest.

"You didn't even sing the songs."

"I will when I learn all the words."

"No, you won't."

"All right, girls. Let's not bicker."

Again, Addie noticed that Mrs. Greene didn't show favoritism. Anyone else would have told Addie to stop *arguing as if she had started it all and had kept it going when that was clearly not the case. Maybe Mrs. Greene wasn't as bad as Addie had thought. Maybe she could get through this week.*

They learned the other fruits of the Spirit that week, including love, joy, patience, and self-control. Carrie made a habit of pointing out which ones she was using. Usually to Addie. Addie didn't care about the fruits of the Spirit, and she didn't care that Carrie knew them well and made them a part of her life.

Addie never had many friends growing up. Everyone seemed to prefer Carrie instead, ever since her first day in kindergarten. That was just one of the reasons Addie hated being so close in age to her sister and living in a small town. The two were almost always in the same classes at church and often at school, especially electives. The circle of classmates was forever the same. And everyone constantly made the same choice of friend: Carrie.

But, there was one girl who hooked up with Addie. Addie was never really sure why. It could have been that Kimberly really did prefer her, or it could have been that Carrie didn't want to have anything to do with Kimberly. Addie thought it was more the latter. Carrie did have an innate ability to read a person within a few minutes. She often told Addie to stay away from someone or not be too quick to judge someone else, and she was usually correct.

However it happened, Addie and Kimberly became fast friends the year Kimberly started attending their school. Addie thought it was nice to have someone to do things with. Someone she wanted to eat lunch with. Someone new who didn't have any preconceived notions about who Addie was.

Again, in her half-sleep stupor, Addie recalled several occasions with Kimberly. There were the times they rode their bikes to the library. Now Addie was not a lover of books before Kimberly, but Kimberly introduced her to a new genre of books Addie had never seen before. Teen horror. It didn't take Addie long to realize these were books her parents would never allow in the house. That made them all the more tantalizing. Kimberly and Addie would check books out of the library on a regular basis and then share them with each other. While Addie couldn't quite explain it, she had some strange feelings when reading some of these books. She may not have been able to define it, but she knew it was exciting in a scary sort of way.

Then the girls discovered they could borrow movies from the library. They found the same types of movies, borrowed them, and watched them in the privacy of Kimberly's room. Her parents didn't seem to mind or see anything wrong with the movies. Her mom would often come in with a bowl of popcorn, a smile, and an "Enjoy your movies, girls!" Some of those movies made Addie inwardly cringe, but she would never let Kimberly know that. Disturbing scenes from a few of those movies still stuck in her head and were no less disturbing even as an adult. Kimberly liked to choose ones with a lot of blood for some reason.

As Addie drifted even deeper into sleep, the dreams kept coming.

"I have an idea!" Kimberly whispered as she and Addie sat at their usual lunch table in the corner of the cafeteria, as far away from the teachers as possible.

"What is it?" Addie leaned in close to hear the secret at the same time she looked around to make sure no one was watching or paying any attention to them.

"Can you come to my house after school?"

Addie made a face. "I can't today. I'm technically grounded." She made another face she knew her parents would file in the disrespectful category.

Kimberly thought for a second. "Wait! You have those

woods behind your house, don't you? Can you meet me there?"

"I think I can sneak out for a few minutes."

"Great! I'll be there around 4:30."

When Addie got off the bus that afternoon, she made a show of going to her room. "I might as well go and do my homework since I can't do anything else anyway."

No one responded. Probably because no one cared. Or because her parents weren't falling for her victim attitude. If they did make any comments, they would have been something like, "Well, if you didn't act the way you did, you wouldn't be grounded." Sympathy, or maybe empathy, was not her parents' strong suits, at least when it came to Addie.

She stomped upstairs to her room, knowing Carrie would spend a few minutes in the living room with their parents, filling them in on the details of her day. If one looked up predictable in the dictionary, Carrie's face would be there.

When Addie heard their voices caught up in conversation, she quietly snuck back down the stairs and out the back door. It only took her about thirty seconds to run into the shelter of the thick woods where her parents would no longer be able to see her. The sound of the crunching leaves sounded loud enough to alert her parents. Addie tried to quiet her rapid steps. Kimberly was already in the clearing.

"Took you long enough!" Her voice sounded upset, but her smiling face said something else.

"Yeah, yeah, whatever."

"Here, sit down." Kimberly gestured to two rocks she had rolled up next to each other and pulled the strap of her cross body bag she carried over her head and opened it.

Addie's eyes crinkled up in confusion when Kimberly brought out a sewing needle. "What's that for?"

Kimberly looked up with a huge grin on her face. "We're going to become blood sisters."

Now Addie was excited. "Like we saw in that movie last week?"

Kimberly nodded her head. "Give me your hand."

As Addie held out her hand, Kimberly took hold of Addie's first finger. She gave it a good poke with the needle.

"Ow!"

"Sorry, but I needed to make sure it was going to bleed enough." She poked her own finger next and squeezed it to make sure it was bleeding. "Here."

Each of the girls held up their fingers and pressed the bleeding parts together.

"How long do we have to hold it like this?" Addie wondered.

Kimberly shrugged. "A few minutes, I guess."

"What are you doing?" Carrie's voice burst into the tranquility of the woods.

Startled, Addie and Kimberly pulled their fingers apart and stood up.

"What are you doing here?" Addie demanded.

"You weren't in the bedroom where you were supposed to

be, so I came out to look for you."

"You're not my mother!" Addie sneered.

"I'm telling Mom."

"Go ahead!" Addie shouted after her.

"I gotta go." Kimberly replaced her bag and turned toward her own house.

"See ya tomorrow."

"Yeah."

Addie wasn't sure why, but Kimberly didn't sound too enthused. She sighed and figured she better get back to the house. Carrie was certain to have told her parents stories of what Addie and Kimberly had been doing in the woods, even if she didn't know the whole truth.

When Addie stepped through the kitchen door, her parents were sitting at the table. It almost looked as if they had been praying, which was weird. Not the actual praying; they certainly did that enough and reminded Addie they prayed for her every day. It was the fact that they were praying in this moment that was a little strange.

"What were you and Kimberly doing in the woods just now?" Dad didn't take the time for any pleasantries.

"Nothing."

Both of them stared her down with a look that made her feel exposed. "We were becoming blood sisters."

"What?" Her mom's voice was just shy of a screech.

Dad was gritting his teeth and probably biting his tongue by the way the veins were popping out on his neck. He grabbed her mom's hand and grasped it hard. "Ellie ..."

Mom patted his hand in silent communication. Dad always acted this way when Addie was in trouble. He didn't want to have to deal with anything concerning her. As usual, he got up and left the room.

Mom took a deep breath and spoke. "I don't think Kimberly is someone you should hang around with anymore."

"Why not?" It was Addie's turn to be almost screaming.

"She isn't a good influence. We know the types of books you've been reading and the movies you've been watching."

"Carrie is such a tattle tale!" Addie mumbled under her breath.

Mom shook her head. "It isn't what you think. Carrie never said a word."

"Then how did you find out?"

"The library called and wondered where the things were you had checked out and were late in returning."

Addie didn't say anything. There wasn't much she could say. But she did curse at Kimberly in her mind for not returning things promptly.

"I want you to go to your room and take the time to research the Bible and see what God has to say about such things."

"How am I supposed to find that?"

Mom shrugged like she didn't care. "Read it. You might also ask your sister if you can borrow her commentary to see *if that will help you find applicable verses."*

Addie didn't wait around for anything more. Standing up, she slammed her chair into the table. "This is completely unfair!" she hollered as she stomped off to her room. She had no intention of asking to borrow Carrie's commentary thing, and she also had no intention of actually reading the Bible. That was stupid. She flopped on her bed on her back and stared up at the ceiling, too irate to cry.

Her parents grounded her for as long as it took for her to come up with some verses relating to what she did. She didn't have a life anyway, so it didn't matter to her, especially since after that day, Kimberly quit speaking to her at school. Yep, Addie was back to not a friend in the world.

One afternoon the following week when she entered her bedroom after school, she noticed a note on her bed. Picking it up, she didn't recognize the handwriting. It was a Bible verse. She read it to herself.

"Finally, brethren, whatsoever things are true, whatsoever things are honest, whatsoever things are just, whatsoever things are pure, whatsoever things are lovely, whatsoever things are of good report; if there be any virtue, and if there be any praise, think on these things" (Philippians 4:8).

Instinctively, she looked around the room to see who could have left it. It definitely wasn't either of her parents' handwriting, and it wasn't Carrie's either. But one of them had something to do with it. Was it her dad? Was this what her mom wanted her to find in the Bible? She knew her parents thought what she had been watching and reading didn't fit into any of the categories in that verse.

As she stared at the card, a plan formed in her mind. Quickly, before Carrie could walk in and see her, Addie sat down at her desk and rewrote the verse. She couldn't very well hand in homework in someone else's handwriting, now could she?

After dinner was over, Addie, as meekly as she could, handed her parents the paper on which she had written the verse. "I found a verse."

Dad read it and smiled, but it wasn't a happy smile. He gestured to the chair opposite him. Addie sat down.

"You found a verse. Do you know what it means?"

"I guess." Addie shrugged.

"Do you think the things you've been reading and watching are any of these things?"

Again, Addie shrugged. But that wasn't good enough. Dad stared at her, waiting for an answer. "I guess not."

"It may seem all innocent to you, but it's anything but. When you allow some of this so-called entertainment into your life, you are opening a door for Satan to come in as well. Is that really what you want?"

Addie didn't know what she wanted. She didn't see the harm in the books she'd read or the movies she'd watched. To her they were simply entertainment, although sometimes disturbing entertainment.

"I'm not saying everything you read or watch has to be strictly Christian, but it shouldn't go against God, either. You need to slam those doors that Satan is trying to use to get into your life. You need to open the one Christ is knocking on and allow Him to come in. Do you understand?"

Addie had gotten lost in her mind for some of her dad's speech, but she did hear the end. She nodded, trying to look remorseful on the outside while she was rolling her eyes inwardly. All she cared about was that the grounding was over. At least for now.

Chapter Six

"Addie?"

Someone was calling her name. She could hear it but had trouble responding to it. She willed herself to move her head, squeeze a hand, moan, anything to let whoever it was know she heard. She was tired of the dream world she had been living in. Finally, her eyes began to twitch, trying to open. How they hurt, whether from the light or from the scratchiness, she couldn't tell. Addie gradually felt the ever-present hand holding hers.

"Addie, can you hear me, honey?"

It was her mom.

"Mom?" Again, her voice was just a whisper, but it was enough for her mother to hear it.

"I'm here. How are you feeling?"

Addie could only shake her head in response. But finally, she was able to ask, "Where..."

She didn't even need to finish the question. Her

mother must have known exactly what she meant.

"You're in the hospital. You've been here for over two weeks now."

"Why?" The one-word questions seemed to be working, so Addie did not even attempt to speak more than one word at a time. It was so hard to inhale and take the breath required for speaking.

Mom didn't answer right away. When she did, it almost sounded as if she was trying not to cry. At least that's what Addie thought.

"You were in a bad car accident. It was a head-on collision."

Addie couldn't muster up the strength to say anymore. She felt herself starting to doze again when a new voice entered the room. This one she had a harder time placing although it was familiar.

"I really need to talk to her."

"Now isn't a good time." That was Mom.

"Do you believe there will ever really be a good time?"

Addie noticed his emphasis on the word "good," but she had no idea what that meant.

Mom started crying. This time, Addie was sure of it.

"No, Chad!"

As soon as she heard the name, Addie was able to match up with the voice and face. Officer Sanders. He had stopped her a few times. If she wasn't mistaken, he was the familiar voice she had heard when her world first went dark.

"There will never be a good time! I'm sorry!" Addie heard her mother's angry voice. She heard her mother's use of the word sorry, but the voice didn't sound sorry at all.

"I need to get this case settled, and it seems like you would want to as well."

"There's no case to settle. Don't you think we've been through enough without the police badgering us every single day?"

His voice softened a little. "I agree that your family has suffered greatly, but that doesn't change the fact that I have a job to do. I need to know what she remembers from the accident."

"She just had a lung transplant. Can't you give her time?"

A lung transplant? Was that why it was so hard for her to breath?

"I understand that, but it doesn't change the situation. The sooner I speak to her, the better."

There was silence for a moment as Mom sniffled. "If she ever regains enough consciousness so she can have a conversation, I'll ask her."

"You know a police officer will have to talk with her anyway. And wouldn't you rather it was someone who knew her?"

Again, the room filled with silence.

"I'll be back tomorrow."

Addie heard the squeaking of shoes on the tiled floor telling her the police officer left the room.

That was one of the last sounds Addie heard as she drifted off into her disturbing dream world again. That and the sound of her mother sniffling and blowing her nose.

As much as she wanted to stay in the real world and get some answers, Addie felt the dreams pulling her away again. Now Addie's dreams took her to the teenage years. Those years are traumatic enough for a normal teen, but Addie was never, quote-unquote, normal.

Addie had found a toy car she could pull back to wind up and then let it loose to go where it might. She wasn't sure where it had come from, but she fiddled with it a few moments, pressing and pulling the wheels across the palm of her hand. Then, looking at it and thinking, a slow smile crept across Addie's face. As quietly as possible, Addie once more pulled the car backward on her hand. Instead of letting the wheels go, Addie held the tires and got up to stand behind Carrie sitting at her desk doing homework. Addie put the car

on Carrie's head and released the tires.

It only took half a second of a mechanical sound for Carrie's hair to be wound all up in the axles of that toy car. At first, she didn't even known what happened. From her vantage point at her desk doing homework, she couldn't see the back of her head.

"Ouch!" she said as she pulled at the stuck car.

"Ooops! Sorry! I didn't know it would do that." Which was partly true. Addie didn't know what was going to happen. It ended up being funnier than she expected.

"I can't get it out!" Carrie started to whine.

Addie's stomach did a little bit of a flip-flop when she thought of what her parents would say when they found out.

"I'll help you. Hold still so I don't pull."

But it pulled anyway. Carrie cried as Addie pulled the hair harder, trying to remove the car. Addie grabbed a pair of scissors from her desk drawer, and with one quick snip, Carrie was free. Carrie turned around, rubbing the back of her head with one hand and her tears with the other.

When she saw the wad of hair and car in Addie's hand, Carrie screamed. "What did you do?" She grabbed the hairy mess and ran to the kitchen where Mom was. Carrie was sobbing uncontrollably.

When Addie was inevitably called downstairs, Mom demanded, "What happened?"

"I'm not even sure."

Carrie still held the car with a twisted bunch of blonde hair that perfectly matched the hair that remained on her head. The scissors were still in Addie's hand.

"Tell her you're sorry."

"I'm sorry."

She wasn't really, but Addie had learned that it was a fast way to get out of a tough spot. Why would she be sorry when she was only helping Carrie anyway? If not for her, Carrie would still have the car attached to her head.

"Now go to your room and think about what you did."

Addie never knew why her parents told her to do that. She would go to her room, but she would never dwell on what she had done, at least not the way they wanted her to. She had done what she did on purpose. Carrie deserved it.

When the girls were young, their parents always made Addie apologize to Carrie when feelings were hurt. Addie couldn't remember a time when they made Carrie apologize to her. Mom or Dad would always force her to say she was sorry. It took her a while to figure it out, but she realized she could say the words without actually meaning them. It made her life so much easier. She supposed she must be a pretty good actress to be able to convince them she was sincere. Once she figured out how easy it was to say the words, she made a habit of it for life. At home and away from home.

Chapter Seven

*A*ddie awoke to the sound of her mother's voice praying.

"Lord, Addie still has a long road of recovery ahead. We all do. Addie's will be both mental and physical, while the rest of us have a lot of emotional trauma to deal with."

Addie used to hate it when her mom said she was praying for the girls. Every morning before school, Addie and Carrie heard, "Hope you have a good day. I'll be praying for you."

Carrie would always go back and give their mother a hug and a kiss. Addie would just roll her eyes and walk out the door, usually without even a goodbye to her mom. Mom would also put notes in their lunches. "I'm praying for you today." "Remember you are loved." These were just a couple of sayings Mom wrote. One time, Addie walked into the kitchen just as her mom was dropping the notes into the lunch bags.

"Stop putting notes in my lunch bag. It's embarrassing."

"Carrie doesn't think so."

"Of course she doesn't. Carrie's the perfect daughter."

"Stop that! If you no longer want the notes, I won't include them."

"I never wanted the notes."

The look on her mother's face showed a little bit of hurt. "But that doesn't mean I'll stop praying for you."

"Don't pray for me. I don't need it. I'm beyond your prayers." The older Addie got, the more she felt she was beyond the prayers of everyone. After all she had done in her life, not even God would want her.

Another biblical picture of Carrie came to Addie's mind. The Prodigal Son, or Daughter. Addie knew the meaning behind the story. No matter what anyone did, Jesus was always in the background, letting people know He loved them. He is always waiting for sinners to turn around and run into His arms.

That picture of Carrie had been stuck in Addie's head for years. Carrie never had any problem running to Jesus. She also never had any problem telling others about Him. The picture left a sour taste in Addie's mouth, but on the other hand, here in the hospital, knowing her mother was praying for her felt different. It didn't annoy her or even make her mad. That was definitely something new. It almost felt ... good? She concentrated on listening to her mother's soft and loving voice.

"She needs you, God. She is going to need You more than ever now. She is going to have to rebuild her life, and I know she is going to kick against that with all she has in her. She knows the truth of Your salvation, Lord, she has just chosen to never accept it. Soften her heart and allow her to hear You knocking. Please, God, send someone to tell her the words she needs to hear. I know that's not me. She hasn't listened to me for a long time. There must be someone who can get through to her. Convince her to open that door and accept You as her personal Savior."

Memories flooded Addie's mind. She really was beyond her mother's prayers, or anyone else's, for that matter. There were so many things she had done simply to be spiteful and hurtful. No. There was no way in the world God would accept her now. Not as she had become. She never meant to be that way; it was just the way she ended up. Even she didn't know why she made the decisions she did. Perhaps that was where all of her insecurities started.

As her mother continued to pray, another thought came to Addie. Where was her father? She had not noticed him coming to visit her. Granted, she had probably been out of it most of the time and maybe just missed him, but she had noticed her mom, the doctor, and nurses, as well as Officer Sanders. Why had her father not come to see her? Her father had never been very talkative, and the two of them butted heads more often than not, but surely she would have felt his presence.

Then Addie's mind wandered back to the negative. Carrie had always been Dad's favorite. Both he and their mom had said it wasn't true and that they didn't have favorites, but Addie was fairly sure they were lying to her. How could they not have a favorite? Look at how her life had turned out! Carrie had graduated from high school at the top of her class with a full-ride scholarship to the college of her choice. Then, just to show off, Addie was certain Carrie graduated from college early, again at the top of her class. The icing on the cake was landing her dream job with a hefty salary. Oh, and now she was engaged to the love of her life. Although Addie didn't know who this mystery man was. Thankfully, she lived on the opposite side of the country, and Addie only had to see her sister during the holidays if Carrie was able to make it home. Even that was something; Carrie had escaped the small town Addie had been so desperate to leave but had never happened. Yet another failure on Addie's part.

Addie, on the other hand, habitually made a mess of everything. She had barely graduated from high school and then flunked out of community college. Now she worked at a factory where no one would notice if she stayed or left. If she weren't there, they would just put a monkey in her place to do the same job she did. She was scarcely able to afford the rent on her one-bedroom apartment in a shady section of town.

Maybe everyone's lives would be better if Addie wasn't a part of them. Maybe she should just give up and die. If it looked like her death was the result of a car accident, there would be no one to blame, and they could go on living in peace, maybe even pretending that Addie had not been real but just a terrible nightmare.

A tear must have fallen from her eye as Addie heard her mother stop praying and focus on her.

Mom wiped the tear away, saying, "Oh, my precious, Addie. What is going on inside? You should be more awake than this by now. What is making you cry?"

Mom then put her head close to Addie's. Addie could feel her mother's tears on her face now. She could cry, and their tears would mingle on her cheek. But, then again, she didn't have the energy or the cognizance for too many tears as she felt herself drifting away again.

∞ ∞ ∞

"Girls? Would you both come here, please?"

Carrie jumped up right away with a "Coming."

Addie took her sweet time. When she finally strolled into the kitchen, Mom asked, "Who did the last load of laundry? A red shirt got in with my brand new white towels, and now they're ruined."

Neither of the girls answered for a moment.

Mom made an exasperated expression that showed she was waiting for one of them to step up and admit it. When neither answered again, she added, "I know it wasn't me, and Dad has been out of town. So, who does that leave?"

Carrie caught Addie's eye. Addie knew exactly what was happening. Carrie wanted Addie to actually tell the truth, but telling the truth wasn't in Addie's nature. She had a hunch Carrie would step up. Addie simply raised an eyebrow at Carrie, challenging her to take the bait.

"I can stand here all night." Mom folded her arms across her chest. "And we all will until one of you fesses up."

With one last sidelong glance at Addie, Carrie said, "It was me. I'm sorry. I must not have noticed the shirt wrapped up in the towels."

Mom just looked at Carrie for a moment. Addie wasn't sure Mom believed Carrie, but Addie certainly wasn't going to correct her.

"I'll buy some new towels with my own money."

Addie didn't think it could get any better!

"You girls go and finish your homework."

Back in their room, Addie gave a smug smile, "Thanks for that. But I hope you don't think I owe you one now. I never asked for your help."

Carrie looked at Addie. "I never asked for repayment."

"There she is, trying to be all Christ-like again. She takes the punishment for something I did, and she doesn't want anything in return." Addie was proud of her snarky comment. She would literally think them up in her down time and store them in her mental locker for later use. And Carrie was never disappointed. There was never too much time from one snarky-comment-needing situation to the next. Addie laughed at her own joke, but she could tell by the look on Carrie's face that she didn't think it was in the least bit funny.

"You know your punishment will never be as bad as what I would get. You should be happy about that."

While Addie was busy laughing at herself, Carrie grabbed her pajamas and her pillow off her bed before leaving the room.

"Where are you going?" she called out mockingly.

Carrie didn't answer.

To herself, Addie said, "Well, you have no right to be mad at me because you chose to take the blame."

Chapter Eight

"Didn't you hear me? I don't want to go!" Addie knew her parents wouldn't have a different answer to her pleas when she shouted at them louder, but she tried anyway. She looked over to Carrie. Addie knew Carrie didn't want to go either, but she was completely quiet on the subject. Typical. Carrie wasn't one to buck the system. That might require disobeying their parents.

Dad shook his head. "I heard you the first time you screamed at me. But you're still going." Then he looked to Carrie to include her in the conversation. "You're both going."

Addie watched as Carrie's shoulders shrank as walked off to her room. Who would have thought Carrie wouldn't jump at the chance to step out of her comfort zone, meet other people, and learn more about God? From everything Addie had heard from the summer camp advertisements at church, it was a place to grow closer to God.

I wonder why she doesn't want to go, Addie thought to herself.

It didn't matter. What mattered to Addie was that she didn't want to go to camp, but her parents seemed to be stuck on forcing them both to vacate the house for a week while professionals came in to refinish the hardwood floors. Addie figured camp was as bad a place as any. What other options did she have?

The week at camp was everything Addie thought it would be. Boring. Stupid. And those games the counselors made them play were so immature. Four times a day, the campers were required to sit through a church service. Addie felt it was bad enough that her parents made her go to church whenever the doors were open. Going four times a day was not her idea of entertainment. And the girls in the cabin ... they were the worst! Every last one of them was so perky and bubbly and nice. It made Addie sick. It was like going on vacation with twenty Carries.

There was one girl from her cabin Addie made friends with. At least as much as Addie could make friends with anyone. Her name was Tara. Tara's parents had forced her to come to camp as well, and the two of them bonded over that. The campers had very little free time, but when they did, Addie and Tara ran into the woods to gripe to each other about everything from the food to the services to the bossy counselors and the too-happy girls. However, they were only at camp two days before the two lost their free time privileges. During free time the third day, they found themselves followed by a counselor.

"I thought we had free time?" Addie asked.

"You do."

"Then why do you feel it necessary to tag along behind us?"

"Since you two haven't come back from free time without being hunted down, you now get me as a babysitter."

Addie didn't like the counselor's snarkiness and allowed that to show on her face.

"You can still go wherever you want; I just have to go with you and make sure you come back at the appointed time." The counselor smiled, acting like she had drawn the short straw on this chore that no one wanted.

From then on, Addie and Tara just stayed on the swings in the center of the camp. The counselor could watch from a distance but not be too close. She still kept both eyes on them, but at least she couldn't hear their conversations.

"I hear there's a big bon fire tonight," Tara said.

Addie shrugged. "Finally, something that might actually be fun."

Tara nodded in agreement. "I wonder if there will be s'mores or hot dogs to roast or something."

"That might be considered fun!" Addie laughed out loud. "We can't allow campers to have any fun around here." She shouted that last part loudly, hoping someone would hear her. But no one seemed to notice. What would it have mattered anyway?

There was one thing Addie knew for sure, and she couldn't even believe she was thinking it: she could not wait to go home. One more day. This had been the longest week of her life.

Later that evening, after dinner, services were held at the bon fire. There didn't end up being any hot dogs or s'mores. The campers were a good bit away from the fire, sitting on logs placed in a circle around the huge blaze. Even Addie had to admit the flames were so hot, it would have been quite uncomfortable to try to toast a marshmallow. Her eyebrows probably would have burned off.

There were no marshmallows, but there was singing. A lot of singing. Since it was the last night of camp, they were going to spend considerable time in service. Besides the songs, the campers were encouraged to give their testimonies or to tell about something that happened at camp that week to help them grow spiritually. So many kids had something to say, and Addie was sure she would fall asleep. Then, a familiar voice caught her ear. It was Carrie.

"I have to admit, I didn't want to come to camp at all. My parents made me. They said it would be good for me, and I would enjoy it. They were right on both counts. I have made some great friends and learned a lot about the Bible ..."

Yada yada yada.

Addie zoned out as Carrie continued her speech. It was all classic Carrie. Everything is good. Everything is grand. Everything is all about God.

Toward the end of the service, the camp pastor asked if any of them had received Christ as a small child. Addie knew Carrie was going to raise her hand. This was her element.

"Sometimes, when we accept Christ as a child, we don't always understand exactly what that means. As we grow in our relationship with Him, we learn more and have a deeper relationship with Him. Maybe there are some of you here tonight who want to renew that commitment and rededicate your life to the Lord. You don't need to accept Him as Savior again; you only need to do that once. But sometimes we need to show God and ourselves that we truly want to live a life filled with Him. We want to breathe Him in and then breathe Him out as we interact with those around us.

"It's easy to want to follow after God while we're at camp. Everything here focuses on spiritual matters. But when you go home, you still need to live a godly life. And it's much harder to do that there with so many negative things coming at you every day. You need to pray and read your Bible daily.

"If there are any of you here who want to dedicate your life to Him, to serving Him, please come forward."

Music was coming from somewhere as many of the campers stepped from their seats on the logs and went up to where the pastor was standing. Those that did joined hands and bowed their heads as the pastor prayed a blessing over them. Including Carrie.

Addie couldn't help but roll her eyes. If Carrie wasn't completely unbearable to live with before camp, Addie was assured it wasn't going to be any better afterward.

Saturday had certainly taken it's time in coming, but it did finally arrive. After breakfast, counselors instructed the girls to pack up all their belongings and clean the cabin. Addie did as little as possible with the cleanup, but she did watch Carrie closely. There appeared to be something different about her. She used to always smile, but somehow, that smile looked different now. Addie didn't want to say Carrie's face glowed, but it did. After a moment of thought, Addie decided Carrie had just gotten some make-up tips from one of the other girls.

Finally, Addie saw her parents' car drive up into the parking lot. She had been sitting there with her suitcase and sleeping bag, just waiting. Mom and Dad weren't even out of the car yet when Addie threw her stuff in the back and got in herself. "I'm ready."

"How about we bring your sister home as well?" Dad asked.

Addie rolled her eyes.

"Are you staying in the car?" Mom asked.

"Yup." Addie was so done with camp.

"Well, we're going to look around and see if we can find Carrie," Mom said.

From her vantage point in the car, Addie could see when Carrie first saw Mom and Dad. She ran up and jumped into Dad's arms, and then she gave Mom a bear hug as well. While Addie couldn't hear what Carrie was saying, Addie knew her sister was talking a mile a minute, if the speed of her lips was any indication.

"Oh, come on!" Addie hollered to herself, flinging her arms up in the air and slapping them down on her thighs as Carrie pulled Mom and Dad into a crowd of people. It was going to be a while. Good thing Dad had put the windows down. Addie needed air and lots of it.

When Carrie finished giving their parents the camp tour, everyone eventually made it back to the car and got in.

Carrie talked all the way home. Addie wished she'd had earplugs. Listening to Carrie's voice was beginning to grate on Addie's nerves.

"... And then at the bon fire last night, I dedicated my life to the Lord."

"Do you think you want to be a missionary?" Mom asked.

Carrie shrugged her shoulders. "I don't know. I guess I'll have to wait and see what God has in store for me. Thanks for making me come. I think it was the best week I've ever had."

Of course it was!

During one of Addie's vaguely coherent times, a movie she recognized was playing on the TV. She hadn't turned it on, so she wondered who had. One thing she didn't wonder about was her feelings about the movie. Oh, how she hated it! It was one of Carrie's favorites, and when they were little girls, Carrie would watch it over and over and over again. Mice singing grated on her every nerve. Addie couldn't see the remote to turn the TV off or the volume down. What she did see was a female custodian dressed in pink scrubs, holding a cleaning rag and swaying to the music. Addie saw the woman's lips whispering the words to the song.

Addie closed her eyes, almost hoping sleep would drag her away from the movie.

∞ ∞ ∞

"Don't you just love this movie?" Carrie asked as Addie sat on the couch with a book trying to ignore the cheerfully singing mice in the movie so she could read.

Addie wasn't successful in her reading because of screeching voices. "No. I hate it!"

"How can you hate it?"

"Easily."

"There's so much love and romance."

"Exactly! You don't think you're too old to watch this over and over again?"

Carrie shook her head. "Never!"

"It turns my stomach."

"How can it turn your stomach? There's true love after all the heartache and mistreatment."

Dad came into the room and started singing along with Carrie, as if the whole scenario needed to get any worse. Addie watched as Dad held out his arms to Carrie, and she jumped up off the couch to go to him. He swirled her around the couch and coffee table, almost knocking the pile of magazines off it. That only made them laugh. Carrie stopped dancing to straighten the mess they made and flopped back down on the couch to continue watching the movie as Dad waltzed out of the room.

He never even looked at Addie. What if she had wanted to dance? Not that she did or anything, but Dad could have at least tossed an offering look in her direction or something.

Nope. He was Carrie's prince, and Carrie was Dad's princess. There was no room for anyone else in their relationship.

If anyone had ever asked Addie, and if she gave a truthful answer, she would have to say that the bad and wicked witches were her favorite characters. She could relate to them. They got the worst treatment and were often misunderstood.

Carrie was good.

Addie wasn't.

Carrie was the attractive one.

Not Addie. Addie's scowl was usually the telltale sign of her ugliness, inside and out.

Carrie did do a lot of the housework, and she did it cheerfully.

Addie would much rather point out what Carrie didn't do or do well enough.

Carrie dreamed of a prince, literal or not, coming to the door someday, sweeping her off her feet, and promising to love her forever.

Addie lived a little closer to reality. Addie never wanted to dream that someone might love her. Dreams and promises weren't worth it. They were meant to be broken.

Yes, Addie definitely related to the bad characters much more than she did to the heroes. She knew life was hard and it would never be easy. It would probably never be good, either. Addie just figured she would go through the motions as she walked through life. She would finish school, get a job, and pay the bills, never getting out of the rut she would find herself in. It was a depressing look at life, but it was what Addie had. And it was hers. No one could take that away from her.

Chapter Nine

*A*ddie felt herself thrashing around in her hospital bed, at least as much as she possibly could with all the contraptions attached to her. Because of all these memories rushing through her mind, Addie was beginning to see Carrie's strengths and her own weaknesses. Addie was beginning to see what a walking testimony her sister had been all these years. Her testimony had been her witness to Christ, and Addie wasn't sure Carrie even knew what a powerful testimony it was. Maybe she had found something Addie hadn't.

It was not any surprise that Carrie had not come to see her in the hospital. Carrie would have flapped her arms and flown across the country for anyone else but not for her big sister. Certainly Addie would have felt her presence since they were sisters and all. But did they really have much of a connection anymore? Did they have any connection at all? Did they ever?

And speaking of feeling presences, she still had not felt her father there. Maybe Addie had been so cruel to them both that they had written her off. Maybe they had no desire to be near her.

At least Mom came.

And the dreams ... they never stopped.

∞ ∞ ∞

"Look at those shoes!" Addie was taunting a classmate who she knew to be exceptionally poor. I'm sure those came from Goodwill ... twenty years ago." Her maniacal laugh reverberated throughout the cafeteria in spite of the noise of a couple hundred other students eating lunch and talking.

The girl, Alison, just lowered her head and looked down at her shoes. They were old, and they had holes in them. Alison tried to walk past Addie, but Addie wouldn't let her.

"Why don't you have your mom take you to a real store for clothes?" Addie knew that comment would be hurtful because Alison's mother had died from cancer just a few months earlier.

That day, Allison was wearing a long, loose skirt that had been in style twenty years ago. The over-bright multi-colors were obnoxious. The shirt she wore was a contrast to the skirt as it was almost too tight, and there was a noticeable stain on the belly, not to mention the stitching on the hem had all come out, leaving the bottom end of the shirt looking ragged.

"Did you buy that skirt because it has every single color in the world in it? So, no matter what shirt you wear you think it will match and look good? Newsflash, nothing can make that skirt look good."

Everyone knew Alison's dad had gone off the deep end after his wife died. He had previously been a good provider financially, but other than that, his wife had taken care of everything. After her death, he had quit his job and started drinking to try and erase the hurt he was dealing with every day. That left Alison on her own. She wasn't old enough to get a job, but she found work doing other things such as babysitting, pet sitting, house sitting. It wasn't a secret in their small community that she liked house sitting the best. That required her to be away from home and her drunken father. He never touched her or hurt her physically when he was drunk, but the mental and emotional stress he put her through was probably much worse. He seemed to forget she had lost someone, too.

Because of a lack of money, Alison shopped at Goodwill for most everything she needed. Some days she wore what must have been her mom's clothes because they hung loosely on Alison's slimmer body and looked ... well ... mom-ish. She had confessed to one of her friends once that it was embarrassing for her to not only have to shop at thrift stores, but to have to wear clothes from there. That conversation had taken place in the school bathroom. Apparently, they had thought they were alone, but Addie overheard everything. Addie then made it her personal goal to take potshots at Alison every chance she got.

"Did you actually bring your lunch today, or is someone else paying for it again?" Addie could go on like this all day, but she knew she only had a thirty-minute lunch period.

Addie felt a sense of satisfaction when she saw tears starting to form in Alison's eyes.

Then, Addie felt someone forcefully push her out of the way.

"Why don't you just leave her alone? What has she ever done to you?"

Carrie.

Figured.

Addie sneered at her sister as Carrie put her arm around Alison's shaking shoulders. "Why are you so buddy-buddy with her all of a sudden?" Before Carrie had a chance to answer, Addie thought of another jab. "I know! You're trying to live out the Bible again! You want to be just like the Good Samaritan!"

It was no secret Carrie took her relationship with God seriously. She made it a daily effort to live as Christ lived and to show His love to everyone whose path she crossed. Because her parents forced her to go to church every week, Addie knew the Bible well enough to be able to throw it back in Carrie's face whenever she had an opportunity.

"Go ahead. Play the role of Good Samaritan today. I'll gladly be one of the 'bad guys' that robbed or walked on by without even a second look!"

Carrie turned with Alison to lead her into a side room off the cafeteria. Addie just stood there with her arms crossed in a stance filled with attitude. She couldn't help but sneer as she watched her sister walk away, trying to comfort Alison. It made Addie so mad that Carrie never raised her voice. Just once it would have been nice to have a shouting match with her sister. Addie figured Carrie knew she could never win that battle, so she never tried. That, at least, gave her a little bit of satisfaction.

But then she couldn't help herself and followed Carrie and Alison. She wanted to pick a fight. And today was going to be that day.

"I wasn't done talking to you!" She shouted loud enough that the entire cafeteria went silent. Addie smiled at the thought that everyone was going to watch her win a fight.

"I have nothing to say to you." Once again, Carrie's quiet resistance was irritating.

Addie grabbed at Carrie and pulled her away from Alison. She heard the gasps from the other students behind her. She also heard a teacher's voice hollering at her to stop and then running in her direction. The cafeteria was big, but it wouldn't take long for the teacher to reach them. Addie had to be quick. She grabbed a hold of Carrie's hair and gave it a yank, bringing Carrie's head down to Addie's knee.

Carrie came up with a bloody nose. If she was lucky, maybe Addie had knocked a few of Carrie's perfectly straight teeth out.

The look on Carrie's face was surprising. There was hurt, but there was something else. Anger? Addie wasn't sure. She had never seen Carrie actually angry before. It took her only about half a second to realize it was definitely anger she saw when Carrie threw her full weight at Addie, knocking her to the ground. Addie's head hit the floor with a sickening thud. She couldn't see for a moment, and it was in that moment Carrie's fist made contact with Addie's face.

That was all that happened before a couple of teachers arrived to pull the girls apart. Carrie was bleeding. And even though Addie was still seeing some stars, she was evilly pleased. She had made her sister livid. Carrie wasn't perfect after all.

Their fight ended up with both of them being suspended. It was the first and only time for Carrie. It wasn't Addie's first, and it wouldn't be her last.

Chapter Ten

Coming out of her stupor, Addie heard voices arguing. Sarcasm in the voice of the male. Anger in the voice of her mother.

"It's time I talked to her."

"I know you need to, but can't you see she is still not up to it?"

"I'm sure that's not what the other driver is thinking."

"You don't need to tell me anything about the other driver."

"Stop!" Addie drawled out the word. She just wanted to sleep. The loud exchange of voices wasn't helping with that. While she did feel a little bit more awake and had a little less pain, she still felt she was struggling with her breathing.

"Sounds like she's awake to me?" That was the male voice. Officer Sanders.

Addie heard her mother let out a long and frustrated

sigh. "Fine." She moved over to the bed and took hold of Addie's hand. "Honey, Officer Sanders is here and needs to speak to you. Do you think you're up to it?"

Addie was not looking forward to another conversation with Sanders. He had it out for her. Always pulling her over just because she was doing two and a half miles over the speed limit. He knew her car and picked her out even though others around her were speeding more than she was.

"Will you be quiet and let me sleep afterward?"

"Sure."

Her mother sounded disappointed, but Addie wasn't sure why. Because all she wanted to do was sleep? Or because she agreed to talk to Officer Sanders, her parents' friend from high school? Another reason to hate small-town living.

Officer Sanders had little man syndrome, at least that's what Addie called it. At 5'6", she towered over him. And he wasn't heavy or muscular in any way, shape, or form. He threw his 120 pounds of weight around behind his badge. Addie often joked that that was why he became a police officer in the first place. He would never appear to have authority anywhere else otherwise. The gun and the uniform gave him the power he desired, at least in Addie's mind.

Officer Sanders stepped closer to the bed and began his interrogation. "Adeline, do you remember the accident?"

"What accident?"

"The accident that landed you a stay in this magnificent resort."

There was that sarcasm again. Why was he always sarcastic with her?

"I don't remember much of anything." The details of the night were rather foggy.

"Do you know where you had been coming from?"

Addie fully closed her half-open eyes, hoping something would come to her. The sooner she told this man what he wanted to know, the sooner she could go back to sleep. "What night was it?" she asked after a moment.

"Friday night. March 15th."

Eyes still closed, Addie wracked her brain for something. A flash came. She saw Ethan's face, smiling at her. They were sitting at a bar, a beer in front of him and a wine cooler in front of her. "A bar?" She phrased it like a question because she really wasn't that sure.

"The Whistler Tavern on Bates Avenue?" The officer asked her a question in return.

Addie squinted, trying to remember. That was her favorite bar, so it was more than likely that's where she was. "Probably."

"Who were you with?"

She had already figured out that answer. "Ethan

Dole."

"How much had you had to drink?"

It didn't escape Addie's notice that he didn't ask her if she *was* drinking. He simply asked how much. "A wine cooler or two?"

The look on his face said he didn't believe her. "Is that all? Are you sure?"

"I'm not really sure about anything." Addie hoped that would help hurry up the interview.

"Your blood alcohol level was more than twice the legal limit."

Addie didn't respond. She knew she hadn't drunk that much. He was probably lying to her, trying to get her to admit to something she didn't do. He wasn't any different than Carrie or her parents.

"Do you remember if you were texting while driving?"

Addie felt like he was trying to get her to say something she didn't want to say. "I told you, I don't remember much of anything."

Looking through some papers on his clipboard, he read some of the texts Ethan had been sending her. "Do these sound familiar at all?"

Addie could tell the content of the texts embarrassed her mother, but like most things, Addie didn't care about another person's feelings. As Officer Sanders read the last text, he held up a piece of paper displaying the photo Ethan had sent.

"Oh!" Her mother blushed and turned her head away.

"Do you remember that?" he asked.

"Vaguely." Addie actually remembered it very well. She remembered that it made her laugh at the time, and it brought a smile to her face now.

"Do you find it funny?" Officer Sanders put the picture away.

Addie didn't respond.

"It's disgusting." She felt he was reprimanding her. "The evidence shows that this was what you were looking at when you veered out of your lane and hit another driver head-on."

A memory of headlights coming at her appeared in her mind. "I was in my lane. That driver was on the wrong side of the road."

"That isn't what the evidence shows. I have pictures of the cars and the tire tracks on the road." He held them up in turn so Addie could see them. All she saw was a mass of twisted metal. Her car wasn't even recognizable. Neither was the other one. "We had to use the Jaws of Life to extricate you from the car."

Addie had no response to that either. What could she say? It sounded like he had already made up his mind about her.

"I think that's enough for today, Chad." Mom had

stepped closer to the other side of Addie's bed.

"I think I have everything I need for now." Looking at her mother, he said, still writing, "Regardless of your feelings on the matter, Ellie, there will still be DUI charges. At least." Then he looked to Addie, slapped a ticket on the bedside table, and said, "See you in court, Adeline." He smiled.

Addie knew he knew that she hated her full name.

"If I have any more questions, I know where to find you." Officer Sanders headed toward the door to leave, but then he stopped and turned around to look directly at Addie. "I find it a little disturbing that after seeing those pictures, you didn't even ask about the other driver."

"I said that's enough for today." Mom was a little more forceful this time, pushing him out by closing the door.

Addie put her hand to her chest. "My chest hurts. I must have hit that steering wheel really hard."

"Your airbags malfunctioned and didn't deploy. You hit the steering wheel. Hard enough to crush your lungs."

"Figures." Addie's fifteen-year-old car was a heap. A rust bucket that barely turned over in the mornings when she needed to go to work. Even her car had let her down.

"As soon as you arrived at the hospital, you had to

have a double lung transplant."

A million thoughts were running through Addie's mind now, but she couldn't organize them into any semblance of order. She felt there were questions she wanted to ask, but she didn't know what or how to ask them.

She began with, "How long will I be in here?"

"Ah, good, you're awake." A nurse had entered the room. "It's time we got you up and moving around."

"I don't want to."

The nurse smiled. "I didn't ask."

More sarcasm. What was it with people?

The nurse pulled the blankets back off the bed. "You've been in that bed for almost three weeks. I want to just get you standing and maybe start by walking to the bathroom and back. How does that sound?"

"Horrible."

She smiled again. "It was a rhetorical question. Swing your legs to the side of the bed."

Addie didn't see she had any choice but to obey, so she did.

"Slowly now. I don't want you to get dizzy."

Sliding off the side of the bed was more challenging than Addie thought it would be. She felt extremely weak, which was unusual for her. Running was one of her hobbies because she liked to feel like she looked good. It gave her no end of pleasure when men gave her a second or third look. Even with her lack of strength, she did succeed in the trip to and from the bathroom, even if with a lot of help. After the nurse got her settled again in the bed, now fitted with clean sheets, Addie laid her head back and closed her eyes. That little bit of exertion was exhausting. She was about to fall into a blessed sleep when a thought came to her.

"Why hasn't Dad been here?"

Mom looked like she didn't want to answer. "Dad hasn't been able to come. Well, he tried to come once that first week."

Addie vaguely felt like she remembered seeing him standing out in the hallway, but then again, everything was all a blur. Knowing he hadn't tried very hard to come see her was hurtful. "I know Carrie was his favorite, but if she were in the hospital, he would make a point of coming to see her." Her father's rejection cut her more deeply than she would ever admit to anyone.

Mom didn't say anything at first, telling Addie it was true. After a few moments, Mom gathered up her things while she said, "It's his story to tell. We all have a story to tell." Without another word, her mom left the room in tears, nearly hitting someone with the door.

"Sorry, Colin," was the last thing Addie heard her

say.

"Time for your meds." Another nurse held up a syringe and a bottle.

Colin. Now Addie knew who he was. He was a friend of Carrie's in school. The little boy she had made cry on the playground because of mismatched socks. Addie never had the time of day for him unless she was picking on him about something. She was fairly certain she had never said a kind word to him her whole life. Perhaps the animosity was because he and Carrie were so close.

Colin certainly looked different. Handsome. Almost. Addie would never admit that out loud. No wonder she hadn't recognized him. During their school years, he was a bumbling mess. He couldn't walk a straight line without tripping over something. He never seemed to be clean—his body or his clothes. Addie recalled one time she asked him what color his hair really was. Since he rarely washed it, it was hard to tell. Addie remembered him being shorter than her, wearing glasses, and having greasy hair. At one point, he had tried to grow a beard, which also ended up dirty. There wasn't a day when he didn't smell bad. Apparently, to try to cover up the body odor he had, he bathed in cologne. The combination was nauseating. Addie remembered smelling him before she saw him. That hadn't been such a bad thing. That way, she could get out of his way and not have to interact with him or smell him up close at all.

But that was then, this was now. Things had changed. Gone were the glasses, more than likely replaced with contacts. His hair was a rusty color, but it no longer looked like it had never seen a bottle of shampoo. The scruffy facial hair was also gone. There was a hint of cologne, but just a hint. Colin looked much more mature now. Like a man.

And he had grown, too. From her vantage point lying in bed, he looked to be over six feet tall. While his lab coat was open in the front, the sleeves seemed to be tight on his arms. Colin's size and strength probably made him an ideal nurse to heft patients whenever necessary.

Fortunately for Colin, he got good grades, probably because he didn't have a social life and got a scholarship to college. Addie hadn't seen him since he and Carrie had graduated high school. And she hadn't missed him or even given him any thought.

Another thing she would never admit out loud to anyone was that he now looked like he could be a character on one of those romance novels she used to sneak into the house and read. A far cry from where he was when they were in school! He was exactly the type of nurse most female patients would dream of taking care of them.

"I don't want any meds."

Without skipping a beat, Colin continued with what he was doing. "If it were up to me, I'd let you suffer. But ... doctor's orders." He stabbed the syringe into her IV with as must force as she imagined he wished he was stabbing it into her heart.

He left without another word.

"No love lost there," Addie commented to herself after he had gone.

It wasn't long before the meds kicked in, and she was out cold, her thoughts drifting back to another memory. This one of her dad. After shave. That smell permeated her dreams.

More dreams. More memories. More anger.

Addie was screaming at her parents. She had been caught cheating at school. It was a class she and Carrie shared, but Carrie hadn't been there to save her this time as she had been sick that day and stayed home.

"I knew this would happen! You hate me! Nothing Carrie ever does is wrong, but absolutely everything I do is."

"We don't hate you." Mom made it sound like Addie's thoughts were ridiculous.

"You can't bring Carrie into this." Dad's voice was

somewhat calm, but only because he was putting so much effort into keeping it that way.

"You were copying answers from another student's paper. What do you have to say for yourself?"

Addie shrugged, thinking the answer was obvious. "I don't remember the teacher talking about it at all in class."

"No!" Dad held up his hand. "You can't blame anyone but yourself." His face was redder than Addie had ever seen it. And then there was the vein popping out of the side of his neck. He was mad.

Addie tried a different approach. "I didn't have time to study, and I didn't know what would be on the test."

"That's part of the reason it's called a test." Mom was getting more and more frustrated.

Dad put his hand on Mom's shoulders. Addie hated that they always stood together. One-on-one, she could take them down, but never when they stuck together.

"This is unacceptable. After your suspension is over, you will have to stay after school every day until you are caught up on all your work. Mrs. Latimer is not allowing you to take the test again since this isn't the first issue we've had. She will give you some extra credit assignments that you can choose to do or not to do. If you do them, she will factor them into your grade. If you choose not too, that zero from the test is going to knock your grade down enough that you might fail the class and have to take it again. Keep in mind, if you have to start retaking classes, you may not graduate on time."

Once again, as usual, dad walked away, leaving Addie alone with her mom.

Dad always knew how to get to Addie. He had once said it was because he was a lot like her when he was a teenager, but she highly doubted he caused as much trouble as she did. She was proud of her "accomplishments." However, not graduating on time was not an option. As soon as she graduated from high school, she could get a job, move out of the house, and never return. That was something she had looked forward to for a long time.

"I'll do the extra credit work." There was no way she was going to prolong the agony of living under her parents' roof any longer than necessary.

"I'm glad to hear that." Mom seemed to be calming down a little bit.

Maybe she could bribe Carrie into doing some of the work for her.

"And don't even think of asking Carrie to do it. I will be able to tell what's your work and what's hers."

Drat! Mom cut her off again.

She stalked off to her room where Carrie was dutifully doing her homework. "I suppose you heard all that."

Carrie shrugged her shoulders. "I wasn't listening. It's none of my business." Carrie had become rather aloof towards Addie, and Addie didn't quite know what to make of it. Getting a reaction of some sort was more satisfying.

She flopped down face-first on her bed. She was so incensed she could have spit nails. Her parents would never accept her the way she was as they did Carrie. Yes. The sooner she could get out of the house, the better.

∞ ∞ ∞

Addie thrashed around a little in the bed, trying to shake herself awake and away from the dreams. It was almost completely dark in her hospital room, even with the shades pulled open, pointing to the fact that it was still night, yet close to dawn. All she wanted to do was sleep, but more memories sparked by the dream flashed through her mind. In September, at the beginning of one school year, Addie thought it was strange that no one spoke to her. At first, she didn't think much of it, and people not talking to her was not a problem, but then she began to question things. One afternoon, after griping that she had to do a science project all by herself because no one wanted to be her partner, Carrie filled her in on a little secret. A secret that was known to almost everyone except Addie.

"A lot of parents told their kids not to be friends with you, that you're a bad influence. Especially after you got caught driving without a license."

"Is that why no one talks to me and everyone is

afraid to even sit next to me?"

Carrie had just shrugged her shoulders.

"Who cares? I don't need them."

She hated living in a small town. Everyone knew everyone else's business. When she thought about it, she was actually surprised the secret had remained unknown to her for so long. Small-town living was not conducive to secrets. They always got out sooner or later.

Addie eventually managed to find a friend or two, but they weren't any better influences than she was.

Chapter Eleven

"It's that time again. You need to get up and moving." The nurse that came into the room was a little too bubbly for Addie that morning.

"I don't want to move."

"Sure you do. You want to get out of here eventually, don't you?" The nurse pulled back the covers from Addie's legs. "We're going to take a shower and get your bedding changed. You'll feel like a new person."

"At least you're not Colin."

"Have you had a problem with him?"

Addie bobbed her head back and forth. "Not really. I just don't like him."

"Hmmm ... a lot of patients request he be their nurse."

Addie's eyes almost rolled all the way back into her head. Gee! She couldn't believe people liked him! Carrie had probably taught him everything he knew. Taking a deep breath and refocusing her thoughts, Addie realized it had been a while since her last real shower. While she knew the nursing staff had tried to keep her clean, there was no substitute for a shower.

"You'll be going home soon, and we need to make sure you can get up and move around by yourself, even if it's just to use the bathroom."

If she were able to move around, maybe Addie would get the privacy she longed for.

Carefully, the nurse helped Addie sit up straight and then swing her legs around to hang off the side of the bed.

"I'm going to let you sit like that for a moment. I don't need you passing out on me. I'll get everything ready for your shower." Again, with the bubbly personality.

Addie was grateful for the pause in movement. The room did seem to be spinning a little bit. It felt almost like that time she had accepted a dare and drank more than normal. What a hangover that resulted in!

The nurse busied herself with grabbing a towel and some clean clothes. Addie wished she could wear her own comfy pajamas, but it looked like she was going to have to settle for a fresh hospital gown.

"Let's give it a try. Take it slow, and if you feel dizzy, tell me."

Slowly, Addie slid off the bed and onto the floor.

Thankfully, she landed on her feet. There was that dizzy again. After another moment, she was able to start taking steps. Her legs felt like rubber after lying in a bed for so long. When she felt she couldn't take another step, the nurse sat her down in a chair she had moved to the half way point between the bed and the bathroom. She hadn't remembered feeling like this the last time a nurse made her get up and go to the bathroom. However, that nurse had helped her a lot more than this one.

"Sit down for a minute. We aren't in any hurry. You need to be able to do this yourself with minimal to no help."

Addie was breathing harder than she ever had been in her life, even after rigorous work or exercise.

The nurse must have realized what Addie's thoughts were. "I know it's hard to breathe. You're going to have to build up the strength in your new lungs. But it will come."

A simple nod of Addie's head told the nurse she was ready to continue. When she finally arrived in the bathroom, she was more than a little pleased to see a bench where she could sit as she washed. She knew she couldn't stand and shower at the same time.

The nurse helped her remove her clothes. When Addie caught a glimpse of herself in the mirror, she gasped. The scars. There was a huge scar that went around and under her breasts from one side of her chest to the other. As she looked closer, she saw that the top part curved up under her arms and around her back some as well. It was lovely.

"It can be a little disconcerting at first, but the scars will lessen as time goes on. Once the staples are out and it's all healed, you can rub some vitamin E onto it to help even more."

As the nurse chatted about how to lessen the scars, Addie's mind wandered.

Who would want her now?

No guy would ever be turned on by this.

When she was finally clean, dressed, and back in bed, Addie was exhausted, but she did feel better. It was amazing how much energy taking a shower took out of her. It was stupid. Showering was something she always took for granted.

"Here's the remote if you want to watch any TV. Use your call button if you need anything. Try and get some rest. Someone will be back in a few hours to get you up and walking." The chipper nurse seemed to just about dance out of the room.

How can people stand to be so ... happy? Addie wondered to herself while sneering at the retreating nurse.

She picked up the remote and turned on the TV. After a few minutes of scrolling through the channels, her head started to bob up and down. She was so tired, but she didn't want to sleep. Sleep was where her disturbed mind became more prominent. Addie wasn't ready for more memories.

But sleep won out in spite of her efforts. The visions that came this time were the most disturbing. They were pictures she didn't know she remembered.

∞ ∞ ∞

"You should see him. He's so cute!" Carrie was telling her mom about a new boy at school.

Addie found that strange since Carrie didn't talk about boys too much. Also, because Addie thought he was cute as well. The sisters didn't usually fall for the same type of guys. One of the side effects of living in a small town with a whopping population of roughly fifteen hundred people, there was not a lot of fresh "meat." The boys they each went to kindergarten with were just about the same boys they would graduate with. Every once in a while, a new face would show up in town, many times leaving shortly after.

But this could get interesting. Addie took her time getting a bowl of cereal, and instead of taking it to her room where she had planned on eating it, she sat down at the kitchen table where she could hear the entire conversation. She would need all the ammo she could get.

"Don't embarrass him or yourself by acting like a fool

around him," Mom was saying. "Take the time to get to know him and just be yourself. If you pretend you're someone else at first, he'll be in for a rude awakening when he really gets to know you."

"I will."

The look in Carrie's eyes was ridiculous. Her eyes were all sparkly like she had never even seen a boy before. Addie rolled her own eyes and shook her head slightly in derision. Carrie was being ludicrous. It wasn't like many boys looked in her direction anyway, at least not the way they looked at Addie. That was one thing she had on her sister. Certainly, the boys probably only looked at her the way they did for one reason and one reason only. Word got around quickly in small towns. But Addie didn't care. It got her the attention she wanted; whether good or bad, it didn't matter.

"I think I'll invite him to come to youth group Friday night."

Addie cringed. Obviously, the little angel would invite someone to church!

"That sounds like a good idea. Do you know if his family has a church home?"

Carrie shrugged her shoulders. "I don't know."

Mom would follow right behind Carrie and invite the mom to something else church related.

"You haven't told me his name," Mom gave a sly smile to Carrie.

"Adam."

Mom nodded her head. "You'll have to keep me posted on what's happening."

The two of them put their foreheads together and giggled like schoolgirls, which Carrie technically was. Addie found their close relationship repulsive.

While they went about their business, Addie's mind went about its own. She was going to introduce herself to Adam. Even though she had seen him in class, she had watched him from a distance and didn't say anything.

The next day at school, Addie found Adam and made a point of making herself known to him. She didn't want to push too hard, too fast, but she thought she made an impression on him.

"So, you're the new guy?" she came up to him and asked.

"That's what everyone keeps telling me." He smiled a smile that left no doubt in Addie's mind why he had caught Carrie's eye.

He had come from California and looked like a typical surfer. Dirty blonde hair, brown eyes, and tan skin.

"You're Adam, and I'm Addie."

"Nice to meet you, Addie." He was gathering books for his next class.

"Where do you have to go next?"

Referring to a printed schedule he held in his hand, he said, "Ummm ... Chemistry. Room 512."

Addie used all the wiles she had. "We're going in the same direction. Can I join you?"

Adam shrugged his shoulders. "I guess."

While Addie wasn't thrilled with his response, they walked together. She chatted about different things going on at school. Then, she turned the topic to him. "What do you like to do for fun?"

"I love baseball. I hope to play for the school team and then get a scholarship for college."

Addie's mind went to work putting a plan into place. "Well, here's your room. I hope I'll see you around."

"Thanks for walking with me. See ya!"

As soon as he was in the classroom and out of her line of vision, Addie turned around and ran as fast as she could to her own classroom, which was in the opposite wing of the school. It wasn't the first time she had lied. Lying came easily when she set her mind on something. She knew she would be late for class, but any reprimands would be worth it.

By the next day, Addie had a plan firmly in place. She caught up with Adam before his chemistry class and walked with him again.

"Want to go to the batting cages Friday night? They aren't too far from here."

Adam didn't answer right away. "I actually already had plans Friday night."

Addie was prepared for this answer because Carrie had mentioned the previous night that she invited Adam to youth group.

"Oh." She tried to sound disappointed. "What are you doing?"

"Another girl invited me to go to her church youth group. They are having some big event Friday night that sounded like fun."

"Who invited you to that?" She hoped her voice sounded sweeter than she heard it in her head.

"Her name is Carrie."

Addie made a face like she just couldn't believe the coincidence. "Carrie is my sister. I was planning to go to the youth event as well. I just thought maybe we could go to the batting cages first and then head to church."

Adam bobbed his head back and forth as if he was thinking. "I don't know. I already told Carrie I'd go."

"Just tell her you'll meet her there. That's where I'll end up anyway."

"I guess it would be all right then."

Addie had him in her clutches. Everything was working out as she hoped it would so far. "Don't mention our outing to her. Let's make it a surprise!" She tried to act as if the surprise would be good.

Adam smiled a little. "Sounds good."

The rest of the week, Addie was on her best behavior. She didn't want to do anything that would screw up her plans. Yes, there would be consequences to pay later, but she was ready for them. Any consequences that came her way would be worth it.

Friday morning, before she left for school, Addie told her mom, "A few friends and I are going to the batting cages after school. After that, we are going to head to church for the Break Out." Hopefully, Mom wouldn't put up too much of a fuss.

"Who are you going with?"

Addie had expected that question. "Lila, Jennifer, and Jeanette."

"All right. Well, you girls be careful. And make sure you call me when you get to church so I know you're there. Dad will pick both of you girls up after the event is over."

"Thanks, Mom. See you tonight."

"Have a good day. I'm praying for you."

Ughhhh! She had almost got out of the house without hearing it. Why did Mom have to say it every single day?

School went reasonably well. There were no major events that irritated Addie. That afternoon, she met Adam at his car in the school parking lot.

"You ready?"

"Yup."

It was just the two of them at the batting cages, so Addie didn't have to share Adam with anyone. She hoped his attention wouldn't be anywhere but on her. While Addie didn't know a lot about baseball, his batting ability was impressive. Adam never missed a ball. Addie, on the other hand, could barely hit one, even after Adam gave her some pointers.

Too soon, Adam looked at the time. "We better be going if we want to get there on time."

Drat! Addie didn't plan to be on time. "Do you mind if we stop and grab something to eat? I'm starving. I'll pay."

"I thought there was going to be pizza tonight at the church?"

Addie shrugged her shoulders. "There will be later, but it's disgusting pizza. And no one washes their hands before touching the food. That's gross after they've been playing games outside and sweating!"

Adam didn't look convinced.

"Oh, come on! It won't take too long, and we can eat in the car on the way to church to save time."

"All right." Adam still didn't sound as if he liked the plan.

When they got to the fast food restaurant that locals knew was notoriously slow, Addie didn't order food straight from the menu. She knew it would take a lot longer to get their order if she wanted something special.

While they waited for their food, Adam kept looking at his watch. He looked nervous. Addie smiled, thinking about her plans to loosen him up in just a little bit.

Just as Addie had intended, they ended up a little late to the youth event. As soon as Adam put the car in park, Addie reached over and grabbed his head. She turned him toward her so she could kiss him full on the lips. She wasn't sure how he would respond but was pleasantly pleased when he seemed to return the kiss. Also, just as Addie had planned, a *tapping came on the window within a few moments.*

"What are you kids doing? Aren't you supposed to be inside?"

It was the overzealous church safety team member, Mr. Harper. He could always be counted on to be there if anything was going on at the church. It was his job to make sure everyone was where they needed to be and stayed safe. If anything was amiss, Mr. Harper would investigate.

Addie tried to act embarrassed and pulled back from Adam. Adam didn't have to try; he looked thoroughly ashamed of himself.

"I'm going to have to walk you in to Pastor Joe." Mr. Harper was so dependable, which made Addie's plan work out perfectly.

Adam and Addie climbed out of the car and walked into the gym where the rest of the youth group would be. Mr. Harper followed on their heels. When she opened the door, Addie felt everyone in the room stop what they were doing and turn to look at them.

To Pastor Joe, Mr. Harper said rather loudly, "These two were in the parking lot ... in a car ..." Mr. Harper seemed to be just as embarrassed as Adam. That made it all the more thrilling for Addie. It was all she could do to hold in her laughter.

Then she caught Carrie's eyes. Adam and Mr. Harper weren't the only ones in the room who were embarrassed. Maybe Carrie was a touch mad as well as embarrassed.

Maybe more than a touch mad. Furious was more like it. Addie sent Carrie a smirk. The look that passed between them said everything spoken words could have said.

Pastor Joe stepped up to the accused couple. "I'm going to have to call your parents. Addie, you know the rules. You should know better."

Without a word, Addie and Adam followed Pastor Joe into the office where it was private and quiet enough to call parents. Within thirty minutes, Addie was stomping up the stairs to her room, grounded for life. Carrie had left the event as well. Somehow, she had managed to hold in her tears until she got in the car. Addie had heard her making a big deal of it to her friends before leaving the church.

"I don't want my dad to have to come back for me. I'm sure he's upset. I'm just going to leave now."

What a saint she is! were Addie's sarcastic thoughts.

As soon as the car doors closed, Dad let Addie have it. "What were you thinking?"

Addie didn't answer.

"I'm waiting."

"I don't know. I guess I wasn't." She lied, chancing a glance at Carrie just to see the look on her face. There was no denying Carrie knew exactly what Addie had done and was not happy about it.

"Your mother is going to have to deal with this. I just can't!" Dad gripped the life out of the steering wheel, that vein bulging out of his neck again. Addie was surprised that *it hadn't burst.*

When they got home, Dad jumped out of the car, slammed the door, and walked away from Addie. Again.

When Carrie came into the bedroom that night, Addie was still awake. "You wouldn't have worked out as a couple anyway. Besides, his kissing wasn't that good."

Carrie remained composed.

That frustrated Addie. Here she had been trying to get to Carrie, make her shout or scream or something. But she remained stoic and unmoving.

Uncharacteristically, a Bible verse came to Addie's mind that she mockingly quoted. "As the sheep before the shearers was dumb, so he opened not his mouth." Then the Golden Rule spilled out as well, "Do unto others as you would have them do unto you." That frustrated Addie, too. Why did she have to think of biblical things when she just wanted to get Carrie's goat? Why did Carrie never react the way Addie wanted her to? Would she ever? Or was trying to annoy her sister a waste of time?

When Addie woke up, she could tell it was the middle of the night by the pitch-black darkness outside and the lack of commotion in the hallway. It seemed strange that the hospital didn't have a lot of outdoor lighting. Maybe it was just the location of her room that didn't allow her to see that lighting.

Everything felt so dark, physically, mentally, emotionally, and Carrie would say spiritually. Addie didn't know why she felt that way. Was it because it was a dark night and she was all alone?

Another thought suddenly came to her. Why had no one come to visit her besides her mom? Not one of her friends had walked through her hospital room door. But then she tried to think of any friends who might have come, and Addie struggled to think of one name. Ethan popped into her head. Where was he? He had been all gung-ho about her at the bar that night. Then again, he didn't even know her last name. All he had was her phone number, and Addie didn't even know where her phone was. Did the police confiscate it? It seemed like they would have given it back after they finished their investigation. She mentally made a note to ask her mom about her phone the next time she came in.

"Do you know what happened to my phone?" Addie asked her mom as they sat silently in the room later that afternoon. Addie couldn't stand that her mom didn't speak much. The quiet was killing her.

Mom pulled it out of her purse. "Yes, I have it.

Officer Sanders gave it back to me after speaking with you. I guess they got all the information they needed."

Mom gingerly handed the phone, which was in a plastic sandwich bag, over to Addie. "Be careful. The screen is all cracked. You'll need a new one."

Addie took it. The screen was shattered. It looked like it did the time she dropped it down the stairs, bouncing off each step as it went. While she could barely read anything through the cracked screen, Addie carefully swiped to open her text messages. There was one from Ethan from that night.

Where are you? Did I offend you with my last text?

She knew his text was laced with sarcasm because there was another picture with a laughing emoji.

But that was it. There were no other messages from anyone asking where she was or how she was doing. She assumed her parents had called in to work for her since there were no messages from her boss either. Maybe he had decided to follow through on his threats to fire her, or maybe he had just hired that monkey to take her place.

So there was the truth of it. No one cared about her. She had no real friends. Then she got stuck thinking about why not. Addie wasn't exactly an extrovert. That was Carrie. Carrie could, and did, make friends with everyone. Addie sneered, recalling the fact that Carrie remembered everything about everyone and always remembered to ask about issues later when someone had shared something personal or a prayer request. Addie never asked about people, and even if someone did tell her about a problem, Addie promptly forgot as soon as she walked away from the conversation. She didn't care and didn't know why anyone would share things with her anyway. Addie was pretty much only friends with people because of what she could get out of them.

Is that how people felt about her? Not caring? Unfeeling? A taker? A user?

It didn't matter. Addie decided she didn't need anyone anyway. She had come this far on her own, and she could continue in the same way. Looking over to her mom, who sat silently in the chair nervously playing with her hands, Addie almost wished she would leave as well. Addie could tell her mom didn't want to be there; that she was only there out of obligation.

"You don't have to stay here, you know."

"I don't mind."

"Mom, I know you don't want to be here. I know you can't stand to look at me. I know I'm not Carrie."

"I have more than one daughter."

"But only one you really love."

Mom sighed. "Don't do this, Addie."

"Do what?" Addie knew she was being hateful, but

she didn't care.

"Maybe it's best if I do go." Mom had her purse sitting in her lap as if she'd just been waiting for Addie to tell her to go. Another sign mom didn't want to be there. "Because it's what you want." She didn't even turn around or say goodbye as she stepped out of the room.

"Finally!" Addie said as the door closed.

But the door had barely closed when it opened again and in walked Colin.

"Oh, brother!"

"I'm glad I'm not." He walked over to the bed where she lay. "I need to check your incision."

"It's fine."

"Are you a trained nurse who can see if there is anything wrong now?"

The derision spewing from his mouth was almost palpable. He hated Addie, and she didn't care. The feeling was mutual

"I'd rather have a female nurse check my incision."

At that comment, Colin raised one eyebrow, and a smirk showed up on his lips. "Why? Are you afraid to expose yourself to someone?"

Addie narrowed her eyes at him. He was one of the few in their small school who had never seen her exposed, as he called it. She never had the time of day for him when they were in school, and apparently, nothing had changed for him. "Is that why you became a *nurse?*" She spewed the vocation out with attitude. "Is that the only way you would get to see a girl naked?"

Colin didn't say anything but instead stared at her. Addie wasn't sure what she was seeing in his eyes. It almost looked like pity, but was it for himself or for her? "It's amazing that two completely opposite people could come from the same parents. Your sister was everything that was good in this world, and you're, well, you're not."

After that, he left the room. Addie realized he never checked her incision. That was fine with her. She didn't want him looking at her anyway.

A few minutes later, a female nurse entered the room. "I hear you're giving Colin a hard time?" She acted like she was trying to be funny, but also that she was on Colin's side. Addie knew what that looked like.

"I'm just more comfortable with a female nurse." That was all Addie could think of to say.

The nurse didn't look like she was buying it, but it didn't really matter. "You have to give Colin a little break. He's been through something tragic lately, and he's suffering. He was told to take time off, but he refused."

"*He's* suffering?" Addie all but spit the words out as

the nurse examined her incision. The ugly scar on her chest was what suffering looked like. "Look at me! I'm suffering."

The nurse said nothing as she inspected the wound, took notes, and left the room.

The art room at school was a haven for Addie, especially during her lunch and free periods throughout high school. Not having many friends, she found she would much rather be alone. But paints, they spoke to her, through her. Art was her escape into a different world. Fortunately, Mr. James, the art teacher, didn't care if she spent time in there as long as there were no classes in session and she cleaned up after herself.

Mr. James was one of the teachers whose classes she enjoyed. Mr. James never told students what they had to draw, paint, or create; he simply gave them a few guidelines and encouraged them to draw what was inside of them. He wanted to see their personalities. Mr. James also never complained about what Addie did create and always pointed out the techniques she had done well.

Through her high school years, Mr. James inspired Addie to follow her dreams. "Don't let anything get in the way of what you want to do." That became Addie's motto and one she took to heart. She never did tell her parents what he'd said; they would probably say she took it the wrong way and to a new extreme. But, sometimes one had to take extreme measures to get what they wanted in life.

Addie collected the supplies she needed: canvas, brushes, and black paint. As she worked, her mind rambled. She knew her parents didn't like her artwork.

"Why don't you draw something wholesome?" Mom had once asked her as she studied one of Addie's drawings of a skull.

Carrie's cringe came while looking at a gothic-looking castle. "The Bible says that out of the heart, the mouth speaks. Maybe that goes for hands, too."

Leave it to Carrie to bring up the Bible and make Addie feel less than. Well, she was less than, less than everyone, especially less than Carrie.

The knife with the dripping blood brought a more positive comment from Dad. Slightly. "There certainly is a lot of detail in the hilt of the knife."

What did they want her to draw? Depictions of stories from the Bible? That just wasn't her at all. And it never would be. Painting was a release from the world she hated. Maybe Carrie was right. Maybe Addie's paintings did speak of the person she was inside. She was dark and brooding. She felt hated by just about everyone. Why should she draw pictures of little girls in pretty dresses running through a field of buttercups? That wasn't real life. At least not Addie's life. Not anymore.

Chapter Twelve

*A*ddie came out of her unconsciousness somewhat when she smelled a familiar smell. As well as she could in her current state, Addie inhaled deeply, trying to grab hold of that fragrance and discover its meaning. Finally, it dawned on her. Dad. Her dad's after shave. Then, hearing his voice, she kept her eyes closed because she didn't want him to stop. She needed him nearby. She needed to hear his voice. She didn't want to make him run away from her again. As she slowly came out of her sleep state, she realized he was speaking to her, not realizing she could hear. She didn't move for fear that if she did, he would stop talking and leave her.

"It was really hard to come today. I hope you don't mind if I don't touch you. I'm struggling with all that's happened. At first, I didn't want to forgive you. Mom told me I needed to, something about you not coming out of things like you should. I don't know. But it wasn't until God got a hold of my heart. I've known about forgiveness my whole life, but it wasn't until the other day that I realized forgiveness was for me and not necessarily just for you."

He paused, and Addie thought maybe he was wiping away a tear or two.

With a breaking voice, he continued. "It's no secret that your mom and I have prayed for you since the day you were born. Even when you told Mom you didn't want her to pray for you anymore, that didn't stop her or me, for that matter. I think I may have prayed too hard. I prayed for God to do something to get your attention. This accident was definitely not what I was praying for, but that's the way things turned out. However, I do hope this is the catalyst that makes you turn your life around. It's never too late to turn back to God. No matter what you've done. He loves you so much. He's already forgiven you for everything you've done; you just have to admit it and confess your sins."

When he paused, Addie hoped he wasn't finished talking to her. In some ways, she felt she needed to reveal she heard him; in other ways, she didn't want him to know. Especially after that whole "turn your life around" bit. She didn't believe in a God who loved unconditionally. She didn't believe that people could simply make an about-face and God would be there, waiting for them with open arms. He wasn't waiting for her. She was sure of that.

"I'll let you get some rest," Dad began again. "I'm still praying for you and will never stop until the day I die."

As he walked out of the room, Addie took a chance and opened her eyes. She saw his retreating back walk out the door. His shoulders were drooping. It looked like he carried the weight of the world on them.

Addie was all hot and sweaty with pleasure. She and her boyfriend she wasn't supposed to have, Todd, were hot and heavy. At fifteen years old and with a constant record of trouble, Addie's parents said she couldn't date until she was eighteen. They told her she needed to focus on her grades at school. She thought it was a ludicrous rule. It didn't seem to be a rule Carrie had to follow, but to this day, she had. Carrie had not seemed the least bit interested in boys beyond friendship, especially after the Adam fiasco. She would rather focus on continuing to get all As in school and be the captain of the soccer team and the star of the drama department. Addie was the complete opposite.

When Addie discovered her parents were not going to be home that afternoon after school, and also knowing Carrie would be at drama practice, she invited Todd over. If her parents knew they were there without adult supervision, Addie would have been in serious trouble. If they knew she had brought Todd to her bedroom, well, life as she knew it would be over. She would be locked in a dungeon and never let out, ever.

But, she would make sure her parents never found out.

When she invited Todd over, she wasn't sure exactly what she expected to happen, then again, maybe she did. Maybe she wanted it to happen. Everything she did reeked of rebellion and went against everything her parents had taught her.

What she didn't expect was for Carrie to come home early from soccer practice. Or to walk in on them. Addie had not heard the front door open and close as she and Todd were too involved with each other and making enough noise to mask any others.

"What ...?"

Addie was only a little bit mortified when Carrie opened the bedroom door and walked in on them in their lust.

"What are you doing?" Carrie had found her voice.

"What does it look like?" Addie took even more pleasure in Carrie's shock. "Get out!"

The look on Carrie's face before slamming the door shut gave Addie no little satisfaction.

In another minute, Addie was pushing Todd out of the house before her parents came home. And then she stood outside the bathroom door, arms akimbo, waiting for Carrie to get out of the shower. As soon as the door opened, she demanded, "You will not tell Mom and Dad!"

Carrie didn't give Addie any more satisfaction when she simply pushed past her, saying, "It's not my secret to tell."

Carrie never did spill the beans on what she walked in on. She also didn't spill the beans a couple of months later when she found out Addie had an abortion. Carrie just avoided Addie at all costs. Even when they were forced to be in the same room together, Carrie would not look Addie in the eye.

Addie told herself she didn't care. They had never had much of a relationship anyway. But as she recalled the memory, Addie felt a twinge of remorse. But only a twinge.

Chapter Thirteen

*A*ddie was finally fully awake after what seemed like forever. No one was in the room with her. She wondered where her parents were now. Actually, she wondered a lot of things. But a nurse interrupted those thoughts when she came in to check her vitals.

"How are you doing today?" she asked. "You're looking a little better."

"I guess I'm feeling better. Breathing seems easier."

"That's good news. Another nurse will be here in a minute to get you up and walking some more." The nurse proceeded to check Addie's blood pressure, heartrate, pulse, and finally, the incisions.

Addie had to turn her head away. She hadn't looked at herself since that first day she took a shower. She found the staples that created a train track of sorts underneath her breasts nauseating.

"Sorry." The nurse must have seen her reaction.

"It's ok." But it wasn't. What had she done to herself?

"It's a shame about ..." she didn't finish her sentence.

Addie didn't have the presence of mind to respond or react as she normally would have. She had no desire for anything.

"I don't see any signs of infection, so that's great." As she packed her things away in a cart, she asked, "Is there anything I can get you? A drink? Something to eat?"

"No thanks." Addie just wanted to be alone.

"Well, ring your call bell if you change your mind."

Addie didn't even nod her head in response.

When the nurse that made her walk up and down the hospital halls was gone about an hour later, Addie rested her head back on the bed and looked up at the ceiling. She wasn't as tired as she thought she might be. The nurse had said she was doing well and could go home soon. Taking as deep a breath as she could without pain, she let it out in a heavy sigh. Her dad's words reverberated through her mind. She didn't need to ask what he meant by turning her life around. It was something he and her mother had been preaching at her for years.

"It's a shame about ..." Addie's head popped up. Out of the blue, the nurse's voice came back to her. What was

the meaning of that? Had the nurse's demeanor changed afterward? While Addie felt more awake, she also felt a little slow in recognizing social cues. Then there was Officer Sanders that Mom kept shutting down, acting like he was going to say too much. Maybe when her mom came in that afternoon, she could ask. Surely Mom would have answers.

But what about the answers to her life? They were not going to be so easy to come by, and no one would be able to answer them for her. Maybe her dad was right.

Interrupting her thoughts, the doctor came in, looking through her chart. "How's it going?"

"That's for you to decide." Addie knew her tone was flippant, but the doctor didn't seem to notice. Or maybe he was just used to belligerent patients.

He laughed a little. "The nurse said she was just in here, and you were awake, so I thought I'd take the opportunity to visit. All your vitals look good. But how are you feeling? Any pain?"

"A little pain. If I'm on any pain medication, I'm sure that's helping to keep it manageable."

"You are, and it must be working. I was hoping we wouldn't have to go to something stronger. I'd like to take a look at your incisions. Is that ok?"

"Sure."

As he lifted the sides of her hospital gown, Addie

had a thought. Maybe he would know answers to at least some of the questions she had.

"What happened?"

"You were in a bad car accident."

"I know that. But I feel like there's something people aren't telling me."

"I'm sure you know everything you need to know." The doctor's voice was softer, and his eyes took on a definitely more subdued look. "All you need to concentrate on is healing. You have quite the road of recovery ahead of you. But you're young and healthy, so you should be fine."

Again, Addie had the feeling he was hiding something from her as well. Knowing he wasn't going to give her the answers she sought, she didn't bother to keep trying. It was too tiring.

∞ ∞ ∞

There was a chill in the air that made it feel more like Christmas time. Now they just needed some snow. Everyone was happy and looking forward to the holiday, except, of course, for Addie. She had never liked Christmas. Her parents had had a three gift rule ever since the girls were toddlers. They bought Addie and Carrie three gifts for Christmas every year. The story behind that was when Mom heard a couple of children at a Christmas party ask, "Is that all I get?" she vowed to never hear that from her children. Christmas was about giving and, most importantly, the birth of the Savior. Yes, the gifts Addie and Carrie received were nice, but there was something wrong about telling the kids at school after Christmas break that she only received three presents. Many of the others got a whole lot more. If Addie had taken the time to think about it, she would have realized that many of the gifts the other children received were cheaper and not the same caliber of gifts she and Carrie received. But spectacular wasn't what mattered; it was the gift count that mattered to school kids.

One evening, in particular, Addie was feeling a little more snide and testy than usual. It didn't help matters when Dad suggested they all go out to dinner and then do their Christmas shopping. Addie had never been a fan of shopping, and that hadn't changed with the teenage years. She didn't have any money to spend on gifts for anyone. Perhaps she would have if she hadn't spent all her money on herself.

"Can I just stay home?" she complained.

"Nope. We're all going." Dad was adamant.

Huffing and puffing, Addie went to her room to change her clothes. She had already put on her pajamas and was planning a night in front of the television.

In the bedroom, Carrie was her typical perky self. It was irritating.

"Don't you just love Christmas?"

"No."

"I do. It puts me in a worshipful mood. I love singing the songs that remind of why we celebrate." She giggled when she added, "Sometimes the songs even make me cry."

Apparently, she didn't get the memo that Addie didn't care.

Carrie kept talking as Addie left the room, unable to handle any more of her sister's cheeriness; she decided to change in the bathroom.

In the car, there was more moping by Addie, but no one seemed to be paying any attention to her. Typical. She put in her earbuds and pulled up her music on her phone. Not Christmas music. And not music the family would all want to participate in singing along together.

Once they arrived at the mall, Mom suggested they split up.

"Why don't you girls go one way, and Dad and I will go another. That way we won't spoil any surprises."

Carrie's cheeriness seemed to have rubbed off on Mom. She smirked to herself when the full gravity of what Mom said sunk it. There would be no spoiling of surprises by her tonight. The surprise would come on Christmas Day when there were no presents for anyone from Addie.

Addie followed Carrie for no other reason than to maybe be a pest. That's what sisters were for anyway. Right?

"I want to go in here." Carrie had turned and was on her

way into a department store. "They will probably have everything I need."

As they browsed through a shelf of clearance items, a sly smile came across Addie's face as she picked up a bottle of shampoo. Addie looked around to see how many people were nearby. The more, the better.

Way louder than necessary, she held up the bottle and said, "Is this what you were looking for, Carrie? It says it's lice shampoo that will help get rid of your lice problem."

People were looking at her with wide eyes. Including Carrie.

"It says right here it will help get rid of your lice in one or two washings."

Addie smirked as people who had been near them dispersed into other aisles of the store.

Carrie grabbed the bottle from Addie and tossed it back on the shelf. "What was that for?" Her voice was a raspy whisper.

"I don't know; I thought I heard you talking about having lice earlier."

Carrie, like normal, held in whatever emotions she was feeling. That always baffled Addie. How did Carrie keep her composure all the time? Addie let her feelings fly no matter where she was or who was around.

Instead of fighting back, as Addie always dreamed she would, Carrie simply turned around and walked away.

"I guess we aren't shopping together anymore tonight." Addie tilted her head back and forth mockingly. While she may not be buying any Christmas presents for her family, the night was a success. She had embarrassed her sister, as only a sister knew how. Embarrassing for the sake of embarrassing, that was a true talent Addie was proud of.

That Christmas morning was a Christmas morning Addie would remember for the rest of her life.

"I made you something special." Carrie handed Addie an exquisitely wrapped gift. Another talent Carrie possessed and Addie didn't.

"What is it?"

"Open it."

The sisters had not been in the habit of buying each other gifts. Well, the truth of the matter was that Addie wasn't in the habit of buying anyone gifts. She could think of much better things to do with the little bit of money she earned at her job at the grocery store than spend it on other people.

Addie was older, and she should have been the one to get a job first, but that wasn't how her life worked out. She wanted to get a job as soon as she was old enough because of the freedom it would give her. Dad wouldn't allow her to get a job because of the freedom it would give her. Dad had said she wasn't responsible enough. There was quite the shouting match that day, but it didn't end well for Addie. As usual. When Carrie was old enough to work, there was no question about her responsibility. Once Carrie got a job, Addie's parents finally allowed her to apply at the same *place.*

When Addie opened the gift, she was literally stunned. It was a quilt Carrie had sewn by herself. What she felt on the inside was not what she allowed Carrie to see. Carrie had used Addie's favorite colors and made a one of a kind, useful present. In a rare moment of sentiment, Addie was touched by the gift. It almost brought her to tears. She had to compose herself before speaking.

"That's cool," she said rather nonchalantly. She was careful not to show too much excitement at the gift. "I didn't get you anything." Addie almost felt sorry that she hadn't bought any gifts. Even she wondered why she was always so mean and thoughtless, but the feeling lasted for only a moment.

Carrie did look a little hurt, but she just shrugged her shoulders and said, "Christmas is about the giving, not the getting."

Addie saw a flash of disillusionment in Carrie's expression and knew she had disappointed her. She saw the same look on her parents' faces as well. Both of the girls had both started jobs that year and for the first time had their own money to spend on gifts. With her first paycheck, Carrie bought a sewing machine with which she could make gifts for others as well as sew costumes for all the school plays. Addie spent her fist paycheck entirely on herself and her wardrobe. She felt that how she looked to other people was more important than buying things for others.

Both attitudes were so typical of their personalities. Carrie was always thinking about others. Addie only thought about herself.

Once again, Carrie had done the right thing, and Addie hadn't.

Each Christmas, Carrie was the one who went all out with everything—the decorations, the food, the gifts, the wrapping, the events, the extra giving she did for others, the extra church services, and worst of all, the Christmas music from morning to night ... every day for the month of December. While their parents went along with it, Addie was not so gung ho. She didn't think her parents could help themselves from getting sucked into Carrie's Christmas Spirit.

"Christmas is all about the birth of the Savior. Why shouldn't we celebrate as much as possible?"

On Christmas morning, ever since the girls had learned to read, Carrie took over the reading of the Christmas story before anyone opened any presents. It was a little extra napping time for Addie. One time, Dad reprimanded her for sleeping when she should have been listening.

"Wake up, Addie! This time is sacred in our home!"

Naturally, everything surrounding Carrie was sacred.

"I wasn't sleeping. I was just closing my eyes so I could visualize in my head what she was reading."

No one believed her story. Even Addie knew it was lame. But after that, she found her mind wandering off and not *listening to the droning on of Carrie's voice a much better alternative.*

Chapter Fourteen

Addie was spending more time awake than asleep now, not that she really wanted to be awake. Yet, sleeping wasn't exactly restful either. When she was awake, her mind went wild thinking of all the things that everyone seemed to be keeping secret about her health. When she was asleep, her mind was flooded with memories of the past.

At one point when she was asleep, she thought she heard her dad's voice again, but she couldn't tell if it was in the present or the past. Everything was muddled. Only when she was conscious was she able to try and sort things out mentally, but even that was confusing and unsatisfactory.

That afternoon, her mother came in. For the first time since being in the hospital, Addie really looked at her and took notice. Mom looked sad and worn in spite of the smile she gave Addie.

"It's good to see you awake when I come in. How are

you doing?"

"I guess I'm doing ok. The doctor and the nurses seem to be happy with my progress. They haven't said anything alarming ... about me anyway."

Mom stopped taking off her coat and looked at Addie. The look on her face told more than she probably wanted it to. "Well, that's good."

It seemed to Addie that Mom was trying to play something off as not important. Addie just stared at her a moment while Mom finished settling herself in for a long visit.

When Mom finally looked at Addie, she asked, "Is something wrong?"

Addie decided it might be good to talk about all that had been going on in her mind. "I've been having a lot of dreams lately."

Mom nodded. "I believe the doctor said that might be one of the effects of the medication. He said some people wake up and talk about the strangest dreams." She tried to laugh, but Addie knew it wasn't a real one.

"But these aren't dreams in the sense that some weird movie is playing in my head. I keep seeing memories. Memories of Carrie and me."

Mom froze at that statement. It seemed to take her a moment to compose herself before she asked, "What memories?"

Addie shrugged her shoulders. "A lot from when we

were kids. Wearing our matching sundresses, eating popsicles, the time she had to get stitches, things at school and church."

Mom appeared to almost cringe at the memories. Addie could tell Mom remembered every single instance she mentioned. Mom looked depressed. But why? Why would Addie's memories bring her mother such sadness?

"Then there were some things with Dad. There were times I couldn't tell whether it was a dream or if he was actually here with me."

Mom nodded again. "He has been here a couple of times."

"Once, I thought he was praying for me."

"Why wouldn't he pray for you? We've all been praying for you. He's been here as much as possible under the circumstances."

New questions shot through Addie's mind. "What circumstances?"

Her mother didn't answer right away.

"Mom, what circumstances?"

The doctor chose that moment to enter her room. "How's everything looking today?"

Addie noticed her Mom send him a slight smile but then back away so he could check on Addie.

"I think I'm doing all right. The nurse had me up and walking around a little while ago. I don't even want to fall right to sleep."

The doctor laughed. "That is definitely a good sign. It means the lungs are taking and healing and that you are able to breathe more normally now. For someone who was in such a bad accident and had to have a lung transplant, I think you're doing great." He patted her on the leg. "If you need anything or start to feel bad in any way, you be sure to tell the nurses."

"I will."

As soon as he left, Addie's eyes returned to her mother, but her mother would not meet her gaze. Instead, she busied herself with straightening things in the room that didn't need straightening.

"Mom, it's my life and my body. What is everyone not telling me? I think I deserve to know. Am I going to die?"

"You're going to be fine." She said it with confidence, but she still wouldn't look at Addie.

"Then what is it?"

Mom took a deep breath and let it out before speaking again. "The lungs you needed came from Carrie."

Addie threw her hands up in the air and slapped them back down on the bed. "I have no doubt they did. Carrie is always the one to be there for people. Carrie always does everything right. Unlike me." For some reason, Addie felt tears of anger come to her eyes. In the past, she didn't care about what Carrie did. Addie just chalked it up to Carrie being the good, little Christian girl she was.

Mom, who'd had her back to Addie, turned to face her with a look of rage. Addie had never seen her mom look that way or exude such hostility.

"Carrie gave you her lungs because you took her life. The other driver, that you never bothered to even ask about, was your sister. You were drunk! You were driving on the wrong side of the road! You killed your sister!" Mom grabbed her purse and stomped out of the room.

Addie felt all the air drain from her lungs. Carrie's lungs. Was it true?

All of a sudden, an image of that fateful night was before her. Addie had been looking down at her phone at the picture and comment Ethan had texted her. When she looked up a car was coming right at her. Both cars tried to swerve, but they swerved in the same direction. Addie could see Carrie's face, plain as day, scared to death.

Now Addie wished she could sleep. No nightmares she'd had were worse than the real life she faced.

What had Carrie been doing here anyway?

What had she done?

∞ ∞ ∞

Prom night. It was a night Addie remembered well, even without the disturbing dreams reminding her.

Addie watched with disdain as Carrie got ready for the prom. Addie was not allowed to go to the prom. She was grounded. Addie made a show of not caring about it at all when the truth of the matter was she had been excited to go. She had seen it as an opportunity to spend some quality time with her new boyfriend. Maybe her parents were on to her schemes. Before the grounding, she had thought up an elaborate plan to make sure Carrie didn't see her leave the event. But all that had changed now, so Addie made a big show of never wanting to go in the first place.

Carrie had spent the past couple of months painstakingly sewing a dress to wear to the prom. Not that Addie would ever admit it to her, but it came out decent. Instead, she spent her time taunting Carrie about it.

"You'll be the only one there wearing a homemade dress."

"Why would you want to spend your time making one?"

"Everyone is going to make fun of you."

"You're going to stick out like a sore thumb."

"People are going to think we're poor and that Mom and Dad can't afford to buy you a real dress."

Through all of it, Carrie never said a word. She just

continued with her sewing. Carrie didn't even comment when Addie teased her about taking Colin, the guy no girl in her right mind would take.

The night of the prom, Addie was sitting in the living room, a plan in her mind. She was biding her time, waiting for just the right moment.

Addie looked up as Carrie made a show of coming down the stairs. Addie could tell Carrie was proud of the dress. And truthfully, she should have been. It was beautiful. It was a floor-length gown. A rose pink lace overlaid a light satin pink underneath. The dress was fitted but still modest with a high neckline halter-top and a slit that came just above her knees. Carrie wore her hair in an elegant braided up do with a few tendrils hanging down on one side to frame her face.

"Oh, honey! You did such a good job! You surprise me every day with your talents." Mom was beaming.

Addie wanted to barf. Carrie was good at everything. Maybe it was because she tried harder than Addie ever tried at anything.

"I'm not sure how I feel about you going out looking like that." Dad teased.

As Carrie stopped on the bottom step, Dad bent down and gave her a kiss.

The way Mom and Dad were gushing over her was sickening. That was when Addie felt it was her moment. She got up, pretending to gawk at Carrie as well. "You look nice." She hoped her voice didn't sound too mocking. That was when she chose to trip and fumble with her cup of grape juice. The cup went flying in Carrie's direction. Everything happened so fast no one had a chance to respond. Not that Addie would have anyway.

Mom gasped louder than Addie had ever heard, and Mom gasped a lot.

"Addie! Watch what you're doing!" Dad shouted.

"Sorry." But she wasn't.

Carrie just stood there for a moment, looking down at what was once a pristine pink prom dress. "Well, I guess I learned my lesson. I should not have been so prideful. The Bible says, 'Pride goeth before a fall.'" With half a smile and a forced laugh, she added, "I just didn't realize someone else might fall. I'm going to go change."

Addie noticed Carrie went up the stairs a little less excited than she had come down.

"Clean up your mess, Addie." Mom didn't holler, but Addie could tell she was disappointed in her and trying to keep her anger under control. It would probably come out as soon as Carrie was on her way.

Dad just stared at her, like he knew she had done it on purpose. And then, as usual, he shook his head and stomped away without another look in her direction.

Addie had just finished mopping up the mess when Carrie came down the stairs in a different dress. If it was possible, she looked even prettier than before. The blue dress set off her blonde hair and blue eyes. The dress was a simple, strapless tulle with a fitted bodice and a full, floor-length skirt that billowed out around her. A belt of sparkling gems showed off her tiny waist and finished the look.

"I'm glad I had worked on this dress a little bit before deciding to sew one from scratch. I had a backup! I can't even say I like one better over the other." She didn't seem the least bit upset.

Which made Addie even angrier.

The doorbell ringing signaled Colin's arrival.

He could have at least showered and combed his hair, Addie noted to herself, taking in his appearance from the top of his greasy head to the hem of his wrinkled tuxedo pants. Was it even a tuxedo?

After the requisite photos, Mom finally let them leave. Addie had watched from a distance. Carrie was still beaming. Why did she always come out on top no matter what? Addie had heard Carrie call that God's blessings before.

Addie just had one question: why was it that God never seemed to bless her?

∞ ∞ ∞

"Hey, sunshine! It's time to get up and moving." It was the female nurse who had come into the room after Addie kicked Colin out, refusing to let him do his job. In fact, he hadn't been back since.

It was then that a little word popped into Addie's mind. *Was*. Colin used that word when he spoke of Carrie. He had known then that Carrie was the driver of the other car. Was her life an open book? Who had the right to tell him anything? She decided to play nice with this nurse to try and get some information.

"So, what's up with Colin?"

The nurse looked at her with a confused expression. "What do you mean?"

"The other day when you were in here, you said he'd been through a hard time lately. What happened?"

She didn't respond right away as she checked and recorded Addie's vitals. "Well, it's not really my story to tell, but he recently lost his fiancé in a car accident. Apparently, she was killed by a drunk driver."

This story seemed to be meshing with Addie's life. "What was her name?" she fished.

"I think it was Caroline or Carrie. Something like that."

Addie suddenly felt as if she were suffocating. Colin was going to marry her sister? No wonder he had treated her like trash. He loved Carrie, so it was no surprise he held absolutely no love at all for Addie.

"Oh," was the only audible response Addie gave.

"Don't tell him I told you."

"I won't."

"Do you need anything? Drink? Snack?"

"No. Nothing."

∞ ∞ ∞

A few days later, Colin showed back up in her room.

"I thought I said I wanted the female nurse."

He held up his hands. "She isn't here today. But don't worry; I'm just checking your vitals. You don't need to worry about your purity or anything."

It was snarky, but Addie knew she would have been the same. She felt what she thought might be a twinge of sympathy. "So, you were engaged to my sister?"

He didn't look at her right away. He took so long, in fact, that Addie wasn't sure if he had heard her. He took a deep breath and sighed as if to compose himself before answering. "Yes."

"I didn't even know you were dating."

"You might have if you had talked to your sister once in a while." The snarky was back.

"Carrie wouldn't have shared information like that with me anyway." She could return snark.

This time Colin did look her in the eyes.

Addie continued. "It's not like a long-distance marriage was going to work out anyway."

"It wasn't going to be long distance. She had

received a job offer here at home and was moving back. When she arrived, we were going to announce our engagement."

So that's why Carrie was in Addie's way on the road and not in Washington State where she should have been. "Maybe I would have found out when I received a wedding invitation in the mail."

"If you got one." With that, Colin left the room.

If Addie could have followed him, she would have. She hated not having the last word.

Another night. Another nightmare. Again, someone was close behind her. As Addie ran, she kept tripping over her shoes. Looking down at her feet, she found the soles of her sneakers were coming loose. Somehow, she knew she needed to keep those shoes on because she was running on some sharp and slippery rocks. The smell of the ocean tickled her nose.

"Addie." The voice kept calling her name but never said anything else. Her heart was beating hard in her chest. It hurt. It hurt to breathe.

When the voice seemed like it was farther away, Addie stopped to catch her breath. Hands on her knees, she bent over, trying to inhale enough oxygen to fill up her painful lungs.

"Addie." The voice was right next to her ear now.

While Addie wasn't typically a screamer, she screamed now. She flailed her arms trying to push away something or someone she could neither see nor feel, and began running again. The voice did not come to her for a few minutes. Maybe she had lost it. Finding a large pile of rocks, she crouched down behind it, trying to calm her breathing. It was so loud anyone within a half-mile radius could have heard it.

Then the voice was behind her. "Addie, I'm waiting."

How did he get behind her? She jumped up and began running again, but it wasn't long before her flapping sneaker completely gave way, and she fell to the rocks.

Addie was awake before her body landed on the rocks that would have sliced her hands and knees as she fell. Holding her hands in front of her face, she inspected them to make sure they were whole with no bloody gouges.

Taking a deep breath and letting it out, Addie tried to calm the racing of her heart. Why did these dreams seem so real? What or who was chasing her? She wasn't sure she wanted to know the truth.

Chapter Fifteen

*A*ddie couldn't stop crying. She was wallowing in self-pity, and she knew it. Her problems were her problems. Her life was what it was because she had made it that way. What about Carrie? Her life had been snatched away from her because of a not-so-loving sister. At least Addie didn't think she had ever loved Carrie, at least not until this moment. Was it possible she did love Carrie deep down inside?

Movement at the door of her room caught her eye. When she looked up, she saw her father. He looked worse than she had ever seen him before. He seemed to have aged several years since she had seen him last, which, while it felt like a lifetime ago, was only really a few days. She quickly swiped at the tears on her cheeks. Allowing her father to see her crying showed how weak she was.

As soon as their eyes met, Dad began sobbing as if

he had been on the verge of tears already. In three strides, he was at her bedside and sat in the chair her mother had vacated earlier that morning. He slid the chair closer to the bed so he could lean on it, but only down near her feet as if he was afraid to get too close to her.

"I came here because I have something to say, and I need to just say it. So let me speak and get it all out." Dad didn't even look up at her face to see if she heard and agreed. Words tumbled out of his mouth with such speed as if he didn't say them fast, they would be gone, never to be spoken at all. "I'm sorry, Addie! Please forgive me. I'm sorry I didn't come to see you as much as I should have." He put his head on his arms at the foot of the bed.

Addie was confused. Forgive him? Why?

He lifted his head and swiped at some tears with the back of his hand.

Addie tried to wave that off like it didn't matter. "I was out of it most of the time anyway. I probably wouldn't even have known you were here."

Yes, I would have. Her thoughts spoke what she truly felt.

"No. You don't understand. I couldn't come and see you because I was angry at you. One of my little girls killed my other little girl."

Addie knew that in his mind, she and Carrie would

always be his little girls. She figured it was some sort of dad code.

"I was angry for the life you've lived. I was angry for all the people you have hurt. I was angry you were the catalyst that took Carrie's life."

It took all the strength Addie had to contain her own tears. She would not let him see her cry even though everything he said was legitimate. She had lived a wretched life. She had walked all over people and hurt them with no care at all, especially if she had something to gain by what she did. Was this remorse she was feeling? If it was, that was something completely new to her.

"But then, God spoke to me. He told me to look at Carrie's life and how she lived it. I should have been her example all these years as her father, but it turns out she was mine. Everything she did was for the Lord. Every decision she made was not made without consulting God. She loved people as Jesus loved them, regardless of how they treated her. She forgave people, even when they had not asked for forgiveness. She knew something that I didn't learn until recently. Forgiveness is not only for the one who did the hurting, but it's also for the one who was hurt."

Listening to him and taking in all his words, Addie wasn't sure that last statement was something she could agree with. Knowing her father had already forgiven her for an unforgivable sin meant a lot. She felt something beginning to change deep down inside of her.

"God had His work cut out for Him when it came to me forgiving you. At first, I didn't want to. I wasn't sure I ever wanted to see you again. All I could think of was all the times you brought pain to our family. But then I realized those memories were tools of Satan. He only wanted me to remember the bad things. When I talked with your mom about that, she brought to mind some of the better memories we all had together. The burden on my heart started lightening, and I could see what God had been trying to show me all along."

Addie sniffled but refused to let one single tear fall.

After a moment, he added, "Ultimately, it was Carrie's testimony that moved me the most. No matter how you treated her, she always forgave you. She would forgive you even now if she were here. I believe she already has from her home in heaven." He grabbed Addie's hand and gave it a squeeze. "I need to get back to work, but I needed to stop in and see you. I know you probably don't want to talk to me right now or maybe ever again, but I had to come and speak my peace."

Not able to speak or even know what to say, Addie simply stared straight ahead at the blank TV.

Dad stopped when he came to the door. With his

hand on the knob, he turned around and gave Addie one last look. "I love you, and I forgive you." With that, he was gone, and Addie was left alone again.

Addie could not hold back the floodgates. These were probably the most tears she had ever cried in her entire life. And these were not tears because she didn't get her own way about something. They were tears for the mistakes she had made. They were tears for Carrie, the life she lived that had been snuffed out too soon. Surely God couldn't love Addie because of all she had done. Growing up in church, she knew what Christ had suffered on the cross. However, Addie was certain Christ had no thoughts for her as he hung there bleeding and dying. There was no way He could have. Addie couldn't forgive herself, so why would He?

As soon as Addie walked into the kitchen one morning, she heard singing.

"Not again!"

That made Carrie sing even louder.

Her life was like a musical. It was not unusual for her to walk around the house singing. Or school. Or church. Or the grocery store. Carrie didn't care who heard her sing. Carrie could be doing any menial task, such as washing dishes, folding clothes, or even vacuuming and could break out in an appropriate song. When vacuuming, she just had to sing louder to be heard.

Conversations were another place where a song was bound to break out every now and then. Someone would make a comment or say something that happened to be a quote from a song, and Carrie would belt out the words with no shame. It was embarrassing. At least to Addie. If they were out in public and Carrie started singing her rendition of some movie chorus line, Addie would lengthen her strides and walk away as quickly as she could in another direction without looking like she was running.

The movie musical songs and even the songs that played on the radio, while annoying as anything, were not as bad as when Carrie started singing worship songs. Oh, how those songs got under Addie's skin! Why did she always have to be singing about God and what He had done for her? Addie couldn't see where He had made a difference in her life. Perhaps that was because she wouldn't give Him the time of day, let alone sing His praises at any given moment.

But the absolute worst was when Carrie was reading her Bible. Almost every single day, Carrie would read her Bible and end up singing about it. How she always had a song to go with every single passage she read was a mystery to Addie, not one she cared to solve, though.

"Why do you have to do that?" Addie had asked once when she walked in on Carrie in the midst of one of her singing sessions; Carrie's eyes were closed, and her hands upraised.

Carrie shrugged her shoulders. "I'm praying. Sometimes the songs other people have written explain my feelings exactly. When I sing, I close my eyes, give God the praise and the glory, and let Him work in my life."

"Oh, I forgot to tell you, I don't really care."

"Then maybe you shouldn't have asked."

It was one of the few times Addie could remember Carrie voicing a comeback, although there was no malice in her tone.

One of the most annoying aspects of Carrie's singing was that those were the songs that then got stuck in Addie's head. All day long. All the time. Addie knew Carrie's schedule and tried to stay away so she wouldn't have to hear and be stuck with a God-song in her head for the rest of the day.

All of Carrie's singing landed her parts in every musical at school. She had almost always had the lead role since they had been in elementary school. Every time a musical was about to open, the newspaper had a story printed about her, complete with an oversized picture. And be on the front page. Once again, Carrie would get all the attention, and Addie was pushed to the side. At least that's how it felt. Carrie on top. Addie on the bottom.

Addie just didn't understand it. Whose life was so happy they always felt like singing? Even Addie knew Carrie's life wasn't that great simply because Addie was a part of it.

One night, Addie overheard her parents talking after they thought the girls had gone to bed. Addie had gotten up to get a drink. When she heard them talking, she stopped outside their bedroom door. Mom was crying, and Dad was trying to soothe her.

"I don't understand why she has to make life so difficult," came Mom's tearful voice.

"I don't know either."

"What did we ever do to her to make her so hateful? What have we done that is so wrong? She doesn't want for anything."

"I know. Honestly, I don't think it's us she has a problem with us. I think it's God in our lives she's fighting against. As far as I know, she hasn't accepted Christ as her Savior."

"I don't know that for sure either."

"And she knows the truth. We have had her in church ever since she was born. We have devotions at home. We try to live in a godly manner. I think it's the Holy Spirit she's in a battle with."

"That doesn't make it feel any better." Mom sniffled. "I want to have a good relationship with her, but I can't if she doesn't let me in."

"I know. All we can do is pray for her and be there for her."

Addie felt like she was in a tight spot. She needed a drink but couldn't get one without walking past Mom and Dad's room. She didn't want them to know she had heard them talking, but she didn't want to stop listening. It had not been a good day. Among other things, Addie had not done her chores and had lied about it. She knew her parents would figure that out sooner or later, but she hoped it would take at least a little longer. Then again, she didn't think they would be upset about a few undone chores. That didn't seem to be something her mom would cry about.

Then, another thought came to her mind.

The credit card.

A few weeks ago, Addie had found a credit card lying on the ground. "Found" being a relative term. The truth was that she had seen a lady drop it while Addie happened to be walking behind her. Addie casually picked it up and shoved it inside her coat pocket. Before the lady could realize it was missing, Addie went into a store. She didn't want to take too much time shopping, but she also didn't want to look like she was in too much of a hurry either. She browsed a little and then grabbed several items before heading to the self-checkout.

Addie briefly looked at a couple more items, but she knew as soon as she scanned them, the computer would alert someone to come and check her ID. No sense inviting extra trouble. It was best to take what she had and leave the store as nonchalantly as possible. Over the next several days, mom noticed her wearing some new clothes, to which Addie had prepared quick explanations.

"I bought the shoes with some birthday money I still

had." "The shirt belongs to a friend at school." While Mom seemed to believe that one, Carrie had no qualms about pointing that out as a lie.

"You have friends at school? I thought you used and abused everyone there."

Addie sighed and decided to go back to her room without the drink. She was too mad to swallow anyway. Did her parents always talk about her like that? Did it make them feel better to gossip and then add a prayer to the end of it? So typical!

And they wondered why she didn't want to be a part of this family.

Chapter Sixteen

After an entire month in the hospital, Addie was finally going home. At least as home as she could go.

"I'm fine to go to my own apartment."

"No, you're not. You need constant care right now. You need to come back for regular checkups for the next couple of months, and you can't drive yet." The doctor argued with Addie. He left the room before she could voice any more opinions.

"You heard him." Dad stepped into Addie's view.

"Well, I'll leave the hospital with you, but you can just drop me off at my apartment."

"Nope."

"Why not?" Addie's voice went up a couple of decibels.

So did her dad's. "You can't lift anything right now. You can barely walk on your own. How do you think you'll be able to get to the bathroom, shower, or feed yourself? Not to mention, you can't work. How do you think you're going to pay your rent?"

"I'll manage just fine."

"You'll manage just fine at our house."

"I don't want to be there."

Dad more or less dropped the suitcase of her few belongings on the floor by the door. He glared at her for a moment before speaking.

Addie knew what he wanted to say. *We don't exactly want you there either.* But he didn't. The deep breath he took must have held that statement in.

"You don't have a car. Even if you did, you wouldn't be able to drive it. Right now, I'm your chauffer, and I'm bringing you home. End of discussion."

She resigned herself to the fact that she had to go to her parents' house for a few weeks at least as she recovered. Who knew when she would be able to return to her own apartment and get back to work. She was feeling stronger, but she knew it would be so easy to overdo it, and then where would she be?

"Fine." She was still not happy about it, but truly what could she do?

The pain caused by moving her body in and out of the car, every bump in the road, and realizing she used her torso to keep her boy upright around every curve made her momentarily forget about her desire to be alone in her own apartment.

"Take it easy, there." Dad was helping her up the stairs to her old bedroom. The one she had shared with Carrie. The one she had not been in for several years.

Mom was standing in the doorway, ready to help if necessary. "There is only one bed in here now so it should be easier for you to move around. Are you sure you don't want to stay downstairs? We can make up the sofa bed in the living room." The look on Mom's face was one of true worry.

"I'd rather be up here." The truth of the matter was that Addie knew she could be alone up here. If she camped out down on the couch, Mom would fuss over her constantly. Then there would probably be that same cold distance Addie had noticed in the hospital when her mom came to visit. It didn't go unnoticed that her mother hadn't visited as much after Addie woke up and seemed to be in the clear. Mom had said she was getting the house ready, but Addie didn't care. She wouldn't have been able to stand the awkward silence in her hospital room anymore, especially since she could stay awake for most of the day with only the occasional dream-filled nap.

Dad helped get her settled onto the bed. Carrie's bed. Addie could tell it was Carrie's bed because Addie had gouged out marks in hers when she was raging one day. They must have gotten rid of it after she moved out. They never even asked her if she wanted it.

185

Figured.

"Do you want something to eat or drink?" Mom was somewhat worrisome, but she also seemed caring.

"No."

"Are you sure?"

"I just want to rest. I'm tired from all the moving around." Addie knew she was short with her mom, but as usual, she didn't care. When she said she didn't want anything, she didn't want anything. Mom didn't have to keep asking.

"I'll bring a bottle of water up just in case you need something to drink while you rest."

"Fine."

Addie knew if she didn't agree to something, Mom would never leave.

After Mom dropped off the water and made sure Addie had enough blankets and the remote for the TV, she finally left Addie in peace. Or not peace. Addie didn't think she had ever felt peace in her life. Now that she was in Carrie's bed, in Carrie's room, arranged the way Carrie liked it, with all of Carrie's stuff staring Addie in the face and accusing her of writing the death warrant for her sister, peace was not going to come.

Addie looked around the room. She hadn't noticed when Dad was helping her get settled, but she now noticed the room was a mess. While there was only one bed, a pile of boxes along one wall made the room feel over-crowded.

What's with all the boxes?

Mom was usually organized and didn't like clutter and messiness. The taped up boxes looked like shipping boxes. Squinting her eyes to try to read the address on one of the boxes closest to her, she saw a Washington State address. It was then she realized what they were. It was all Carrie's possessions. Her parents must have had all Carrie's belongings shipped to them. But then Addie remembered Colin saying Carrie was moving back home. Maybe Carrie had sent them since she obviously wasn't going to be living in Washington anymore. Or anywhere else for that matter. Those boxes may as well have been Carrie herself sitting there staring at Addie and reprimanding her for another mistake she had made.

Maybe watching a little TV would help take her mind off things. Addie flipped through the channels but was soon frustrated when it seemed that her only choices were a musical or a church service. Absolutely everything that popped up screamed either about God or Carrie. Neither were appealing right then.

Turning the TV off and tossing the remote to the nightstand, Addie thought about sleep. She lay back as much as she could and tried to close her eyes, but they kept popping open. Addie was not in the least bit tired, in spite of what she had said to her parents. Her body may have been in need of stillness, but her mind was running wild.

Reading. Yeah, she could read, even though she was never much of a reader. But Carrie had been a lover of books, surely there was something close by Addie wouldn't mind reading. However, the only books she saw in easy reach were Carrie's Bible and journal. While perusing the books on the shelf, Addie found an old Bible of Carrie's. Addie picked it up, remembering this was a gift in their Easter baskets one year. Addie had a matching one. Well, almost of matching. At least they were matching when they received them. Carrie had actually used hers, and it was well-worn. Addie's ... not so much.

Carrie's Bible was falling apart. It looked like she had written in every spare space on each page. Some sections were highlighted. Others seemed to have some type of color-coding where she used colored pencils. The binding was falling off, and some pages had been taped in place.

"I don't know why she insisted on using this old thing when she could have bought a new one." Addie tossed it aside with a thump, some of the pages spewing out. Addie glanced toward the bookshelf where the matching Bible had sat ever since Addie received it. As a child, she would remove it from the shelf or church on Sundays when her parents reminded her she needed to take it with her.

Addie walked over to the shelf on the opposite side

of the room, the one that contained her Bible, and pulled it down. The spine cracked when she opened it. Yup, it was not as well used as Carrie's. It looked brand new. There was quite the layer of dust across the top of the pages from just sitting on the shelf. She replaced her Bible in its spot.

Going back to Carrie's shelf, she browsed the books there. These were the ones Carrie must have decided to leave at home and not take with her to Washington. But Addie knew without a doubt Carrie had taken her Bible. She thought it was funny that Carrie's Bible and journal were unpacked when nothing else was. Mom probably did it on purpose. The Bible was definitely out of the question for pleasure reading, but the journal might be good for a few laughs. Addie picked that up and chose a random day.

Lord, Addie needs You. She doesn't realize it, but she does. I need You as well. I need You to help me when it comes to my reactions to her. She infuriates me, Lord. I don't understand why she feels it necessary to do things just to be spiteful. Today, Mom made her water the plants. My essay for English was sitting on the counter, and Addie made a point of spilling water on it. It wasn't that big of a deal because I had typed it out and saved it on my computer, so all I had to do was reprint another copy. But it's the fact that I know it wasn't an accident that upsets me. This is what my whole life has been like with her. Of course, You know that, God. You created us both. You made us sisters for a reason. I pray that You would help me see that reason and be loving and kind, even if she isn't in return. Forgive me for being so angry with Addie. I'm trying to love her as You command, but I would be lying if I said it was easy.

Addie put the journal down in her lap. Maybe picking up the Bible would have been better. At least she wouldn't read about herself. Resting her head back on the headboard, Addie sighed deeply.

Mom chose that moment to enter the room. "Are you okay? Do you need anything?"

Addie tried to toss the journal to the side before Mom saw it, but she wasn't successful.

"Do you really think you ought to be reading Carrie's journal?"

"Do you honestly think she'll care?" Addie's words were biting.

Mom shrugged her shoulders. "I guess that's a decision you'll have to make for yourself."

Her mom was getting good at returning the biting words. This was the second time Addie ever remembered it happening–just now, and the one time in the hospital. Maybe she'd just had enough of Addie's attitude, but as usual, Addie didn't care. Was there ever a time when she cared about anything?

"There's something I wanted to talk to you about, but I'm not sure how to bring it up. It's a little bit of a sensitive subject." Mom was doing her nervous hand-wringing habit.

"Just tell me what it is." Rip the bandage off. Whatever Mom had to say, Addie was sure she didn't want to hear it. The quicker Mom said the words, the better.

"Have you thought about counseling?"

Addie made a face of confusion. "Why would I get counseling?" This subject had come up more than once throughout her life. Her parents thought she needed counseling because, in their words, she had anger issues. All the times before when they had suggested counseling, Addie had angrily declined. Oh, the irony! They tried making her go once when she was a teenager and still living at home, but while in the counselor's office, Addie refused to say a word. Without anything to go on, the counselor couldn't offer any help to anyone in the family.

"If she isn't going to talk, there isn't any sense in bringing her back," the counselor had said. "I can only help those who see they have a problem and are willing to try and work through it." He had said this in front of Addie, probably trying to hurt her feelings and see the error of her ways. It didn't work.

After that one session, her parents never forced her to go again. They did try to go about it a different way when they said, "If you ever feel the need to talk to someone about anything, you let us know, and we will get you the help you need."

Yeah. That wasn't going to happen.

Now Addie wondered what Mom's purpose was. "Why would I need counseling?"

"Because of the car accident."

"People are in car accidents every day."

"But not everyone ..." Apparently, Mom had trouble saying the words.

"Kills their sister?" Addie had no problem finishing her mother's sentence.

Mom looked at her with anger, or was it pity in her eyes? "You don't have to be so callous about it!"

Addie shrugged her shoulders. "It is what it is. I can't change anything now."

That must have been the last straw for Mom as she got up and left the room, slamming the door behind her.

Addie wasn't sorry the conversation was over.

She decided to try once again to sleep. Sleep was healing, right? And the faster she healed, the faster she could be back in her own apartment with her own life. But after tossing and turning as much as she comfortably could and without being able to rest, she sat up. Carrie's journal was taunting her from the floor where Addie had dropped it. What else had Carrie said about her? Not being able to resist, Addie painfully reached for the journal and opened it up to the back.

I don't understand her, God! Why does she have to do what she does? She never takes anyone else's feelings into consideration! She never thinks of anyone but herself! I'm so tired of trying to be nice. I'm tired of trying to be a godly person. I'm just tired, I guess. Where do we go from here, Lord?

Even though Carrie never mentioned Addie's name, Addie knew she was the one Carrie was tired of. Being tired of life wasn't exactly an unknown feeling to Addie either. Maybe the sisters did have at least one similarity. The only difference was that Carrie was tired of life because of Addie.

This time when Addie tossed the journal, it was to make sure she never saw it again. It landed in the garbage can with a thud.

"What a bunch of trash!"

∞ ∞ ∞

"All rise," the bailiff said as the judge entered the room. "The first case on the docket today is Commonwealth versus Adeline Denton."

"Are all the parties present?" the judge asked.

"Yes, Your Honor," Addie's public defender

answered promptly at the same time Officer Sanders did. Addie didn't even glance in his direction.

For some reason, Addie felt naked standing there alone beside her lawyer. It was as if she had been stripped bare for all the world to see. She didn't like it. Crossing her arms in front of her, she tried to cover up as much of herself as possible.

"Please stand respectfully, Ms. Denton," the judge reprimanded.

Addie's arms dropped to her sides with a huff.

"I don't allow attitude in my court room, young lady."

Not knowing what to say, Addie just stood there. Once again, her actions were misinterpreted, and she was tired of it. Did this judge talk to other people about the case before Addie even got in the room? Startled out of her reveries by her public defender subtly stepping on her toes, she said, "Sorry, Your Honor." There was still a little bit of attitude in her voice.

The judge looked up at Addie and gave her a thorough gaze before glancing back down to the papers in front of her. "This case looks cut and dried." Looking back to Addie, she asked, "How do you plead on the charges of driving under the influence?"

Addie wanted to say not guilty because she knew she could have safely driven home. It was that Sanders that had it out for her. The public defender, in a brief meeting yesterday afternoon, had suggested how she plead. "Guilty."

"Those are the only charges I see before me today. I am ordering you to pay $1000 in fines and take a driver's safety course. By the looks of these pictures, you no longer have a vehicle; however, I am ordering that when you do get a new vehicle, an ignition interlock be installed, but your license is suspended for twelve months. Your parents may want to consider having the interlocks installed on their cars, but I won't order that right now. If I feel it necessary later, I may. I imagine that takes care of any driving restrictions your doctor may have already given you."

Addie rolled her eyes. Even the judge had it out for her.

"Also, because I know the other facts in this case, I am ordering you to get some counseling."

Addie shifted her body in a posture of attitude. She may also have rolled her eyes, but she did that so often it was hard for her to tell. Until the judge spoke again.

"And, because I don't like the attitude you are showing in the court room today after what you've done, I am going to order you to a hundred and fifty hours of community service. I think the women's shelter would be a good place for you to see what your life might be like one day if you don't straighten up."

What in the world? Addie tried to control the emotions

that were raging within her. This was too much! She didn't have any money to pay the fines. Now she couldn't drive for a year? How was she supposed to get a job to pay the fines? And what was she supposed to tell any potential employers? "Sorry, I can't work today. I have to do community service."

After Addie was allowed to leave the court and she and her mom got back in the car, she crossed her arms over her chest and stared out the window. Fortunately, her mom didn't say anything all the way home.

Chapter Seventeen

*A*ddie thought the dreams would stop once she had left the hospital. But no. Could anything be more perfect for Carrie? Addie's snide remarks managed to stay inside her head. Carrie had gotten the lead in the school musical ... again. Just before the performance, Carrie found out that a professional theater company had a representative there to watch her, possibly to offer her a job or admission into a special theater program after graduation. Carrie's dream was to teach drama in a high school somewhere. It would probably work out great for her. Everything else did. Besides, she had been doing dual enrollment in college for the last couple of years. She would graduate with her Associate's Degree before she got her high school diploma. Only two more years at the most for the overachiever and she would be able to teach anywhere she wanted. Yup. Everything always worked out for Carrie.

"Golden Girl!"

"What?" Mom leaned over and asked.

The auditorium was a little loud before the musical started with five hundred people talking.

"Nothing." Addie hadn't meant that to be spoken out loud.

But that's how Addie saw Carrie. The Golden Child. The one who did everything right. The one who had to work hard at nothing. The one who had everything go her way. All the time.

Addie settled in to take a nap when the lights went down in the auditorium, signaling the beginning of the musical. However, there was so much music and dancing that sleep was not possible. All Addie could do was watch her sister do her thing and do it well. And then, at the end, watch everyone applaud Carrie with a standing ovation.

Yup. Carrie had it all.

After the musical was finally over, Addie and her parents waited while Carrie changed out of her costume and greeted all her fans.

"You have a very talented young lady," more than one person said as they walked past.

"Thank you!" Mom and Dad were beaming. They were so proud of Carrie.

Why aren't they proud of anything I've done? Addie grudgingly wondered.

What have you done? A voice that wasn't her own, forced its way into Addie's head.

The voice was disturbing enough that Addie tried to

nonchalantly look around and see if someone had actually said it out loud. But she saw no one. At least no one that was paying any attention to her or talking directly to her. Not even her present teachers, who stopped to congratulate her parents on what a good job they were doing with Carrie, took notice of Addie. There was never any mention of Addie or even a smiling glance her way. She was the older sister. Wasn't Carrie supposed to be in Addie's shadow? Life was certainly backward.

Addie was an average student. Granted, she did as little as possible when it came to schoolwork. She wanted to just get through, not really caring whether she passed with flying colors or just simply passed. Grades were not as important to her as they were to honor student Carrie.

Yup. Everything Carrie touched became golden.

"Addie, it's time for your physical therapist to come. Do you want to work in up here or downstairs?" Mom asked, walking into the bedroom with a basket of laundry on her hip.

"Do I have to do it at all?"

"You know what the doctor said. And the harder you work, the less time you'll probably have to do it."

Yeah. Work hard. That was what Addie was all

about. "I don't want to do it."

"That isn't what I asked. I asked if you wanted to do it up here or downstairs." Her mom was pulling no punches today.

Addie let out an exaggerated sigh to show her displeasure over the entire situation. "I guess I'll come downstairs. At least it would be a change of scenery from these four walls." Which seemed to be closing in on her.

Mom helped Addie navigate the steps. At one point, Addie wished her mom would just let her go so she'd fall down the steps and maybe end this nightmare.

By the time Addie was situated on the couch in the living room, the doorbell rang.

"Don't get up." Mom was trying to be funny, but Addie didn't see the humor.

As soon as Mom opened the door, Addie heard her let out an exclamation. "Oh!"

"Hi, Mrs. Denton."

As soon as Addie recognized Colin's voice, her eyes rolled back in her head. Oh, brother!

"Addie is in the living room. I'll leave you two be."

"Irony is grand, ain't it?" Colin said as he came in and set down his bag of belongings.

"I thought you worked at the hospital?"

"I was getting some experience under supervision. Now I'm on my own and get to come to people's homes. And here I am. God must be punishing me for all the bad things I've ever done."

Addie knew he wasn't any more thrilled about the situation than she was. "You could have said something about a conflict of interest."

"I'm trying to build up my career, not tear it down. Tearing things down is your area of expertise. Now, we both have jobs to do. I'm going to do mine and push you hard so you can move on with your life. I don't want to hear any whining."

"Don't be so dramatic. Let's just get this over with so you can leave."

"Sounds like the perfect plan to me."

In this dream sequence, Addie recalled something unusual. She had been walking down the stairs to get a snack when she heard Carrie crying.

"I don't know why I did it?"

Addie stopped short. This was definitely a conversation she wanted to hear. Was her perfect little sister not so perfect after all?

"Why do you think you did it?"

From her vantage point, Addie could see Carrie shaking her head. "I have never done anything like that before in my life. I don't know what possessed me to do it. I am so ashamed of myself!"

This was intriguing! What could Carrie have done that

was so bad? Smirking to herself, Addie guessed that whatever it was, it was nothing compared to some of the things she had done. Carrie was probably upset for leaving the water running while she brushed her teeth or something stupid like that. Dad often fussed at the girls about their wasteful water usage. She continued listening to the conversation.

"How do you feel now?"

"Horrible! I feel horrible!" Carrie all but screamed.

Whatever she did, Addie thought it must be a death sentence in her sister's mind.

"I'm glad you feel bad."

Addie grinned when she heard her mom say that. It was good for Carrie to get knocked down a peg or two.

"Feeling bad means you have regrets. If there's no regret, there can be no repentance."

Drat! Addie should have listened to the rest of what Mom had to say before being overjoyed at a non-existent rebuke.

"Oh, I am certainly feeling regret!" Carrie was still bawling.

"What do you think you ought to do next?"

Mom and Dad were always ones to make Carrie and Addie figure things out on their own. They never told the girls what they should do. Instead, there was a lot of conversation about what the girls were thinking and feeling and how they could remedy any situation they were in. Carrie seemed to thrive because of these conversations.

Addie just found them annoying and a waste of time. Perhaps that was because she didn't regret much of what she did, even if Mom and Dad saw it as an offense to themselves or someone else, especially to God.

Addie heard Carrie take a deep breath and release it. "I need to go talk to her and apologize."

Addie was back to smirking. So there was someone Carrie did something to!

"Then I will go to God and ask for His forgiveness as well."

Addie was eye-rolling once again. Carrie always had to turn everything around so it ended back up at God.

"I think that's the perfect solution, but don't be surprised if she isn't willing to forgive you at first. Accept her feelings and opinions, but let her know you are sorry. Even if she doesn't, you can know you did the right thing. On the other hand, you can be assured that God will forgive you when you speak to Him."

"Thanks, Mom."

"Anytime, sweetheart."

Now Addie felt the need to gag. Their mother-daughter relationship was sickening.

When she heard the scraping of Carrie's chair as she got up and started walking toward the stairs, Addie stepped back up a couple and acted as if she were just coming down.

"Hey," Addie said as Carrie passed

Carrie said nothing in response.

Addie knew her sister was completely distraught over

whatever it was she had done.

So, she isn't perfect after all!

Addie had a smug smile on her face for the rest of the day.

Addie sat up in bed as quickly as her healing torso would let her. She was sweating and breathing hard. Taking a deep breath, she let out the air through lips formed into an O. What was that? She knew there had been a dream but was hard pressed to remember what the dream had been about. The one thing she knew for certain was that the dream was disturbing, otherwise, she would not have woken with such a start or been sweating and breathing heavy. She put her hand on her chest, hoping to somehow slow her heart rate from the outside of her body.

Seeing the remote on the nightstand, she turned on the TV hoping to find something mindless to watch as she allowed her body to settle down to normal.

"We have a high pressure system that's settled over us this week, so everything will remain calm," said a weather girl on a local news channel.

Addie snorted at that thought. A calm front may have settled as far as the weather was concerned, but there was certainly not a calm front in her life right now. Her life was the exact opposite of a calm front.

After flipping through enough of the channels to realize there was nothing even remotely interesting to watch, Addie turned off the TV and slowly got out of bed. She knew she needed to move around more to build up her strength so she could eventually move back to her own apartment, and sooner rather than later. She didn't like the feel of her parents' house. It was strange. It was unsettling to her. She would never have been able to explain it if someone asked; she just knew what she felt.

Having the first twinges of hunger and thirst she remembered feeling for a long time, Addie slowly made her way to the kitchen. Something smelled sweet, similar to her mom's company coffee cake. She and Carrie had always called it that because Mom only made it when company was around. Stopping in her slow steps, Addie wondered if Mom had company. If she did, Addie did not want to see anyone or be seen. Continuing toward the kitchen, she crept as quietly as she could just in case there was someone there.

It wasn't long before she heard voices.

"Well, God has different ways of speaking to us."

"That's the truth!" That was her mom's voice. Addie was uncertain of the other one.

"I know sometimes I pick up the Bible and feel as if God is speaking to me directly. Other times, He uses people to confirm something I've already been thinking about."

"I know exactly what you mean. Sometimes I'll be out in public, and the strangest feeling will come over me. It's almost like there's a voice inside me giving instructions for something I'm supposed to do. There have been times I've felt led to buy a person a meal."

That was not an uncommon thing for Addie's mom. Addie could remember countless times they had gone to a drive-thru and purchased an extra meal. When they would ask her about it, Mom would just say, "God is telling me that someone needs to eat." Sure enough, there would always be a person standing along the side of the road or sitting alone in a parking lot that Mom was able to pass a bag of food to.

Carrie had picked up that habit as well.

Addie, not so much. She had better places to put her money. If someone wanted food, all they had to do was get a job and buy their own.

The other woman's voice spoke again. "My grandmother was adamant about her dreams being some special signs from God. I don't know how much I believe that, but I guess God can use all sorts of things to communicate with us."

That thought brought the dream back to Addie's mind. She still couldn't remember what the dream was, let alone be able to discover a meaning behind it.

Was God trying to speak to her? Shaking her head, she removed that thought from her mind. She had never felt God's presence in her life before, and she was sure He wasn't trying to talk to her now, either.

Deciding it was best to quietly go back up to her room, Addie grabbed an apple that sat on the table next to where she stood eavesdropping. That would have to be enough of a snack. It took her a few minutes to get settled by herself, and when she was finished, she was breathing heavily. It still hurt somewhat to breathe still, especially when she tried inhaling deeply. She was tired but not tired enough to sleep.

Leaning her head back on the headboard, she closed her eyes. As soon as she did that, a picture flashed through her mind. It was from the dream. She could barely see it, but not clearly enough to figure out what or who was in that picture. Try as she might, she could not pull it up from the recesses of her memory.

"Maybe doing something else will help." Addie picked up her phone and started searching the Internet for information on dreams. Some of the sites she found were just plain weird, but then she stumbled onto one that talked about God speaking through dreams. A lot of the information was about the Bible and how God used dreams to speak to biblical characters. Even though there was a lot of Scripture, Addie kept on reading.

Many people in the Bible experienced dreams when God was speaking to them. Daniel did when he dreamed about end times. God sent Peter a dream when he was debating on what foods he should and shouldn't eat. Joseph had all sorts of dreams that opened his eyes to his future and the future of others. Jacob dreamed and wrestled with God because he was afraid. God wanted him to see that He was available at all times and He will stand by us in our times of need and fear.

Addie read of others whose dreams were recorded in the Bible. Maybe there was something to the idea that God spoke to people in dreams.

Now, if only she could remember what that dream was, then she might be able to figure out what it meant.

∞ ∞ ∞

"You have a visitor," Mom said as she came uninvited into Addie's room.

"Who?" Addie knew she didn't have any friends that cared about seeing her. It wasn't her normal PT day, either. And Mom wouldn't have called Colin company.

"Pastor Townsend." Mom didn't exactly shout out her answer.

"Why?" was Addie's next question. Why would he want to come and see her?

Mom let out a frustrated sigh. "Can you just come down and visit for a few moments? And without attitude, please? This is part of his job. He visits members of his church who are ill."

Ill. There was a funny word to use. Addie wasn't exactly ill. Neither was she a member of the church. If her memory served correctly, members had to make a confession of faith, get baptized, and then go before the church to be voted in. Addie had done none of the three.

Addie felt it best to appease her mother in this. "Fine. But I'm not staying down there long. I can fake not feeling well once I get bored with him." Which Addie didn't see taking more than five minutes.

"Hey, Addie!" Pastor Townsend stood up as soon as Addie walked into the living room. "You're looking much better since I saw you last in the hospital."

Irreverent Addie made an appearance. "I didn't know you'd come to the hospital."

"I try to visit all our members who are in the hospital. Some days I feel like I spend all day there."

Addie didn't respond as she made herself comfortable or at least made it look like getting comfortable was difficult. That was part of her effort to make his stay last no longer than a minute and a half.

"So, how are you feeling?"

"I've been better."

Mom gave her a disappointed look as she took that moment to walk into the room with a tray of lemonade.

Smiling toward Pastor Townsend, she said, "There are good days and bad days. About like anything else I suppose."

"I bet," Pastor Townsend remarked. "But you're young and healthy. I'm sure it won't take you too long to get to feeling like your normal self."

Addie cocked her lips and raised her eyebrows in derision.

"Well, let's get to the crux of why I'm here."

That would be great! Addie thought to herself.

"The court ordered you to get some counseling for a variety of reasons. I have the necessary credentials, so I am who your parents chose to try and walk you through all that you've been going through."

It was then Addie noticed that the tray of lemonade her mother had prepared only held two glasses. Her mother must have noticed Addie's observation because she got up and started to leave the room.

"Well, I'm sure you don't need me here for that, so I'll leave you two alone."

Addie didn't think she had ever seen her mom run away from anything so fast in her entire life. She shook her head in disbelief.

"I'm sure you have definite feelings about me being

here in this capacity, but I truly do want to help you. I've known you and your parents for a long time, and you're all like family to me."

Addie doubted that.

"I thought today we could just get to know each other a little better. Maybe you could give me some ideas of things you'd like to talk about. I also want you to know that over the next several months—"

"Several months!" Addie struggled to stand up as fast as she could, depending on her arm strength to get her fully up.

Pastor Townsend held up both his hands. "Addie, the issues you have didn't happen overnight, and the problems won't be solved overnight. I want to be here for you to help you get through this."

Addie gingerly sat back down when she really wanted to flop down as hard as she could to make a statement about her feelings. But flopping would only cause her physical pain. And the courts had ordered this stupid counseling. If she wanted to be able to get her license back, get a job, and move back out on her own, she needed to comply. Checking all the boxes the court had ordered would allow that to happen, whether she benefitted from it all or not.

"So," Pastor Townsend began, "is there anything specific you would like to talk about, either today or in future sessions?"

"Not really."

"Well, I'll start then."

Pastor Townsend droned on and on about things he had witnessed in her over the years, mainly her anger issues. He more or less politely mentioned her drinking and carousing. "I can tell you've been searching for something and that you've been searching for a long time. I want to help bring that to the surface so you can deal with it. I'll be right beside you the entire way."

No one had ever supported Addie the whole way through anything, and she didn't expect that from this pastor-turned-counselor. However, she had goals, and he could help her get there. For the next hour, she answered all his questions the way she thought he might like her to answer them, although his frequent note taking irritated her. Why did he have to write everything she said down? Was he going to study her later?

"Before we end today, I want to leave you with a few verses. I'll read them, but I also wrote them down for you on these index cards so you can keep them near to you and read them whenever you feel you need comfort.

"The first one is Job 33:4. 'The Spirit of God has made me; the breath of the Almighty gives me life.' God loves you so much that He put His own breath in your body to give you life."

Addie thought that sounded a little bit strange and weird. What did God come down from heaven and give her mouth to mouth or something? But she decided to keep those thoughts to herself.

"The last verse I want to read is Ezekiel 37:5. 'This is what the Sovereign Lord says to these bones: I will make breath enter you, and you will come to life.' You are precious in God's sight. It is He who gave you life, and it is He who wants to see you live well."

He handed the cards to Addie. She took them with the intention of tossing them in the garbage can. She didn't need this high and mighty man revealing what he thought were her problems with the objective of solving all of them. Did he think he was God? Did God even want to solve her problems? Probably not.

As Pastor Townsend got up to leave, Mom popped back into the room. *She must not have gone very far,* Addie thought to herself. Addie assumed her mother had been listening.

"I'll see you same time, same place next week. If you think of anything you want to talk about, write it down and have it handy."

"I'm sure she will," Mom answered, smiling, probably figuring Addie wouldn't say anything. "Thanks for coming and being there for us."

Addie was up in her room before her mom closed the

front door and pretended to be sleeping when she came upstairs. Mom had heard it all; she didn't need a recap from Addie.

Chapter Eighteen

Addie was tired of just sitting around the house. She had been able to get up and move a little more each day, but she needed some fresh air. She needed other people in her life, except for her parents. She needed to get away from parents who prayed for her morning, noon, and night. The house felt creepy, as if there were eyes everywhere, watching her every move and not allowing her to be free. Picking up her phone, she sent a text to Ethan.

Hey! Sorry I have been MIA. Bad car accident. Hospitalized. Surgery. Wanna meet 2night?

After a few minutes, a ping signaled a response.

Who's this?

So much for that idea. She tossed her phone down on the couch. Since she had to get a new phone, she had lost all her contacts. She blamed that on her dad. He thought buying her a new phone was a good idea, a peace offering of sorts. He kept her old number, but didn't transfer her contacts. Unfortunately, Addie didn't know any of her friends' numbers off the top of her head. She had to look up Ethan's, which she knew now to be a waste of time. Apparently, everyone had forgotten her number as well. She had yet to receive one call or text since the accident. Didn't anyone care about her or wonder where she had been?

Maybe she just needed to go out and make some new friends. Yes, that's what she was going to do.

Wait. She didn't have a car.

"Mom? Can I take your car out this evening?"

Mom walked into the room. "Did you forget your license is suspended?"

"I'll be fine. I'm not going far. I just need to get out for a little while. I'm going stir crazy."

"Well, where would you like to go? I'll take you anywhere you want. I didn't hear the doctor give you the go ahead to drive yet, either."

"I was thinking of a bar to meet up with some friends."

Mom just stared at her for a moment. "Really?"

Addie stared back.

"I'm not taking you to a bar."

"I didn't ask you to take me."

"You're also not taking my car to a bar. Do you remember what happened last time you were out at a bar? Your father and I took the judge's advice and installed the interlock systems on our cars."

Would she never live the accident down? Every time she wanted something, her parents felt it necessary to remind her of what she had done. She remembered! She didn't need to be reminded every single day.

"Never mind." Addie stomped off to her room, at least stomped as much as she could without jarring her body and causing pain.

There was no one she could call and ask to pick her up. Then she had a thought. Her parents liked things this way. They wanted to keep her down. They wanted to keep her under their thumbs for the rest of her life. Well, that wasn't going to happen. It was going to change as soon as Addie could make change happen.

She needed to call her insurance company to make sure things were moving along with her claim so she could get another car, move back to her own apartment, and get on with her life.

"Yes, this is Addie Denton. My policy number is 496853. I am calling to find out how my claim from my recent accident is going."

"Let me look you up," said the woman on the other end. "Oh, you should be receiving a check for $1000, the value of your car. You will also be receiving a letter stating that we will no longer be able to insure you."

"That's ridiculous! Why?"

"You were at fault for the accident, and because you

were driving under the influence, we cannot retain your policy."

"But only $1000 for my car?"

"That was the Blue Book value."

"It was worth way more than that."

"You can file a dispute if you disagree. You can do that on our website—"

Addie didn't hear the rest of what the woman said as Addie had hung up. Now, she was enraged! Could her life get any worse? She had no car and no means of buying a new one without being able to work for a while and then only getting $1000 for the car she wrecked. Stuck. That's what she was. Stuck in her parents' house. Stuck in a dead-end life. On the bright side, if there was one, she had the money to pay her fines now. Addie lay on her bed staring up at the ceiling for so long she didn't realize she fell asleep.

∞ ∞ ∞

"I am so excited!" Carrie was just about bouncing off the walls ... literally. She hopped from one foot to another, hands clasped in front of her chest.

"I can see that, Tigger!" Mom commented on the bouncing.

"There's so much to do between now and then. Letters to

write, money to raise, stuff to buy, clothes to pack—"

"Whoa! Whoa! Whoa!" Mom held up a hand to stop her. "Can I please read this in peace?" She waved the letter Carrie had handed her as soon as she walked in the door after youth group that night.

"Sorry!" Carrie whispered, covering her mouth with one hand but still bouncing.

When Mom finished reading, she said, "It sounds like a great opportunity. What about you, Addie? Are you interested in going on the mission trip as well?"

Addie snorted. "Umm ... no!"

"I think it would be a good experience for you."

"Not interested in the least."

While Addie said she wasn't interested, she hung out in the kitchen a little while longer, taking an exorbitant amount of time to fix a snack so she could hear the conversation between her mom and Carrie. Carrie was sure to get some kind of special treatment from all this. She always did.

"Well, we need to talk to your father first. I do think it's a great opportunity for both of you. I remember when I went on a mission trip as a teenager. It made me see how much differently other people live and helped me appreciate what I have."

Addie knew there was a message for her in there somewhere. Addie was sure Mom didn't direct it at Carrie since Carrie was always grateful for everything. She even took the time to write down things she saw as blessings in a "Blessings Journal." Addie often felt the need to make fun of *that. She had found Carrie's book once and read through it. Definitely good for a laugh.*

"What a blessing the rain is today! I know it will help the spring flowers bloom and summer crops flourish."

What? Carrie hated rainy days. It was like when the sun wasn't out, she didn't know how to act.

"Today, I'm thankful for answered prayers. God, You know who I need in my life and who I don't."

Addie wished she knew the story behind that entry.

Carrie's Blessings Journal was full of stuff like that. Yet another thing to make Addie want to throw up in disgust.

"Are you sure you don't want to go?" Mom's voice brought Addie back to the present.

"Definitely."

Over the next few months, Addie watched as Carrie worked hard to raise the money she needed to go. She sent out letters to friends and family asking for donations. She babysat whenever she found an opportunity. She did extra chores around the house that Mom and Dad would pay her for. Addie didn't understand why she worked so hard. After it was confirmed that Carrie would be going, Mom and Dad said they would pay whatever money she needed that wasn't covered by what she raised herself. Addie couldn't believe it! Carrie was getting a free vacation.

One night, as they were preparing for bed, Addie saw Carrie pull out her money for the mission trip to count it. Addie hadn't realized Carrie was keeping all that money in their room. Why wouldn't she put it in the bank or something where it would be safe? A fire could burn down the house and her money along with it. A robber could break in and steal that wad of cash. Or a sister.

It was too easy. Addie didn't even know what she would do with that money, but she was sure something fun would pop into her head sooner or later.

The next day, when Carrie was babysitting, Addie saw her opportunity. She took the money out of Carrie's nightstand and hid it in another spot. Addie wasn't sure if she would actually spend the money or not, but it was going to be fun to watch Carrie sweat a little.

She was not disappointed.

"Where's my money?" Carrie yanked the blankets off a sleeping Addie later that night.

Addie rolled over, reaching for the blankets as the air felt cool. "What money?" she asked sleepily.

"You know what money! The money for my mission trip!"

"I have no idea."

"Yes, you do! You're the only one in this house who would take it."

"Maybe Mom and Dad put it in the bank. It's stupid to keep it in your nightstand."

"How did you know it was in my nightstand?"

"You pull it out and count it every night!"

"I know you took it. Where is it?"

Dad came bursting into the room, the door banging against the wall. "What's going on in here?"

Carrie whirled around and put her hands on her hips. "Addie took the money for my mission trip, and now she won't tell me where it is."

"Addie, where is the money?"

"Why do you think I had anything to do with it?"

Dad just looked at her with an exasperated look on his face. To Carrie, he asked, "When did you last see it?"

"Last night. I was counting to see how much more I needed."

"Well, no one extra has been in the house since then, so I don't think we were robbed." He looked to Addie for an explanation.

"I told you I don't know."

He acted like he might have been starting to believe her.

"Carrie, are you sure you put it back in your nightstand?"

"I was pretty sure."

Addie hid a smile under her blankets as she watched Carrie start to second-guess herself.

"Is there anywhere else you would have put it?"

Carrie stood there thinking for a moment, shaking her head. "I don't think so."

"We should have insisted you put it in the bank."

Addie hid another smile under the blankets.

Suddenly, Carrie forcefully shook her head. "No. I'm positive I put it back in the drawer of the nightstand. That's where I've kept it from the beginning. I haven't ever put it anywhere else."

Dad looked back to Addie for an explanation.

"I told you I don't know." She said the words slower this time. She could show exasperation, too.

"Well, it's late. We'll talk about this more in the morning."

Dad left the girls to themselves.

The last words Carrie spoke were, "I know you took it." She slapped at the light switch harder than necessary as if to emphasize her point and close the subject.

Addie was just glad to go to sleep.

She didn't think any more of the money for a few days, at least until Carrie was getting ready to leave for her trip. Addie thought it was a good time to mess with her sister.

"I guess you found all the money you thought was stolen. I told you it wasn't me."

Carrie stopped folding her shirt long enough to look up at Addie and glare a little bit, but then she went right back to what she was doing. No matter what Addie said, she couldn't get a rise out of Carrie for anything.

"Did you forget where you put it?"

Nothing.

"Did Mom put it somewhere safer for you?"

Nothing.

"Did the burglars come back and return it?"

She at least got a will-you-please-shut-up look with that question.

When Carrie was finally off on her trip, Addie thought everything was all over, and the money was hers. But she was wrong.

As soon as she and her parents walked back into the house after dropping Carrie off at church, Dad pointed at the couch and demanded, "Sit!"

This was weird, even for Dad.

She sat.

He leaned over and got as much in her face as he could. "I don't know what you did with Carrie's money, but we weren't going to let you ruin this trip for her. While she's gone, you're going to work your tail off to make up for all we paid."

Addie swallowed hard.

"And the work is going to start now. Out in the garage, you'll find plenty of totes. You're going to organize the garage today. And you're going to do it to my specifications. If it's not, you'll continue working until it's done right. You won't eat until it's done. Tomorrow, there will be other chores. Don't make any plans this week."

Dad pushed off the arm of the couch as if it took everything in him not to take a swing at her. He had never hit them in anger, but Addie felt like he was teetering on that edge. She knew he was serious, and she decided not to make any comments.

Dad took the week off from work so he could watch her every move. While she would have dilly-dallied doing some of the chores, as soon as she began to slack off, he was on her like he had never been before. She dropped into bed each night absolutely exhausted. Addie didn't think she had ever worked so hard in her life. But it was worth it in her mind. She had two thousand dollars stashed away, and no one knew where it was.

But then, at the end of the week, the day before they picked up Carrie, Dad came into the bedroom and sat on Carrie's bed, which creaked under his weight. He stared at Addie without saying a word.

Finally, Addie couldn't stand it anymore. "What?"

"I know you took that money, and I want you to hand it over right now."

"I didn't take her money."

Dad stared.

Addie stared back.

"I can do this all day."

Addie thought she could, too.

"I have another week of vacation coming. I can take next week off."

Addie finally gave in. She knew it was no use to hide the money anymore. Her parents would be watching her like a hawk until that money showed up somewhere in the form of clothes or something else Addie wanted to buy. She sighed as she turned to her closet. After digging through some of her dirty laundry, she pulled out the envelope Carrie had put the money in and handed it over to her father.

Dad looked like he was going to get all sentimental. Looking Addie in the eye, he said, "You're your own worst enemy. You know that, right?"

Addie didn't respond.

He started to walk out of the room but turned and added, "We will not be discussing this with Carrie, ever."

Addie was almost afraid of what would happen if she did. She decided she just wouldn't talk to Carrie at all. Or her parents.

As Addie came out of her slumber, she hated everything and everyone, including herself. She was tired of these dreams. It was as if her life was flashing before her eyes.

Suddenly, a new reality dawned. Had Carrie only been trying to protect her all these years? Had Carrie been trying to save her from unnecessary pain? Was she her own worst enemy? Had she finally gone too far?

Maybe her parents were right; maybe she did need counseling. Would Pastor Townsend have anything to say about her dreams? Maybe she'd ask him. Maybe.

"Hey, Addie, can you come down here, please?"

Addie rolled her eyes as she heard her father's voice calling to her. Didn't he know that she would rather be left alone to wallow in her misery? As she walked down the stairs, which she noticed was getting less and less tentative, she couldn't help but see the grin on her dad's face. He looked like a kid in a candy store or like someone who had a great secret he couldn't wait to share.

"You need to come out to the garage. I have something to show you."

Probably my packed bags so they can kick me out of their

house, Addie thought.

When Dad opened the door to the garage, Addie saw an old, rough-looking piece of furniture. Was this what he was so excited about?

"Okay ..." Addie drew out the word, showing she didn't understand his excitement.

"I had this brilliant idea! I was driving home from work and saw this sitting on the side of the road. As I passed it, I remembered all the amazing things you used to make in shop class and thought maybe you would like to try your hand at refinishing it. I don't have the space and the tools that your shop class had, but I don't have to park my car in the garage so you can have a place to work on it. I figured you could fix and resell it since you're not able to work outside of the house yet. You can work on it a little at a time as you feel up to it. You could make a little money for yourself."

Addie's emotions were circling madly inside of her as she looked over the piece. She was surprised her dad had thought about this for her. Shop was a class Addie enjoyed for more than one reason. The first reason was that a lot of the boys hung out there. There were very few girls, so the odds of getting a guy were in her favor. Number two, she found she was good at working with her hands. It was different than her art classes. There was a lot to be said about taking a pile of wood planks and making them into something beautiful and serviceable. She could never tell anyone how she felt about working with the wood and seeing the finished product. That might make them see her as weak. And she was anything but weak.

She remembered when she brought home her first finished project: a framed mirror with hooks to hold coats, hats, or whatever. Her dad had seemed truly impressed with it and hung it right by the back door where they always entered the house. It still hung there to this day. Addie recalled that being one of the few times she felt as if she had accomplished something worthwhile. There were several other projects she made throughout her high school career, but that all stopped when she graduated.

However, she was unsure of whether this was a project she wanted to work on or not. She was livid, thinking that her parents wanted her to make money so she could move out as soon as possible. She also wanted to give her dad the biggest hug she ever had since she was little for thinking of her and for giving her something to do to pass the endless, boring hours.

"Thank you." She wasn't sure of what else to say. But she didn't need to worry about that. Dad was filling up any empty silence with his own words.

Stepping to the shelf on the other side of the garage, he held up all the things he had bought as he mentioned them as if he were a kindergartener during show and tell.

"Here's a big drop cloth you can put on the floor to protect it. Here's a can of stripper with some foam brushes. Here's an electric sander with some sand paper. I got some special gloves that will help protect your hands from the chemicals. A scrapper. And some masks. Make sure you wear one while you're working to protect your breathing."

His excitement was almost rubbing off on Addie. She still didn't know what to say, but she managed another "Thanks."

"I can't wait to see what you do with it." Mom was standing behind her with a smile as big as Dad's.

"When you're ready, we can go pick out paint or stain or whatever you want to do with it. We can get new knobs as well." Dad stopped talking but still had a huge smile on his face. He was proud of himself and his idea.

And ... it wasn't a terrible idea.

"Do you want to get started on it right away?"

Addie wasn't sure she would have been allowed to say no without a fight. "Maybe."

"Well, we'll leave you to it," Dad said, walking past her and quickly brushing his hand down her arm. It was a gesture of love that Addie hadn't felt in a long time. It was nice, yet she was confused about how she should feel.

"I'll let you know when dinner is ready," Mom said before closing the garage door and leaving Addie to herself.

She walked over to the cabinet to get a better look at it. Someone had painted it. It had drawers and doors and was quite a bit taller than a table. Maybe an old buffet? The door fronts had ornate carvings. The drawers pulled out easily and seemed to be in good shape. The top looked a little rough. There were circles where people had carelessly set sweating drinks without using coasters. It was in rough shape, but the bones were good. With a little bit of elbow grease, Addie thought she could restore it to its original beauty. Surprisingly, she couldn't wait to get started. And she didn't wait.

Grabbing a rag, she rubbed it over the surface of the buffet to remove any dust and loose dirt. Next, she filled a small bucket with warm, soapy water and scrubbed away the thicker grime that would be difficult to strip off. When she was done with that, she stepped back to inspect her work. Anxious to see the wood underneath, Addie spread on a coat of stripper and let it sit for the suggested period of time. With one scrape afterward, she could see the beautiful wood.

"Why do people paint over amazing wood?" she said out loud to herself.

After one coat of stripper, Mom poked her head in the garage. "Dinner's ready."

"Coming."

Addie went inside to wash her hands before she ate. She even sat at the table with her parents. She felt almost happy, like things were as they should be, at least a little bit. This was a first for Addie.

Dad still had that silly, schoolboy grin on his face

when he sat down. "Do you think you'll be able to do anything with that?"

Addie nodded her head. "I think so. I already gave it a good scrubbing and started stripping it."

"You let me know if you need anything else, and I'll get it for you."

"I will."

"Do you think you're going to paint or stain it?"

"Definitely stain. It's tiger maple, and I don't want to cover that up with paint."

"I can't wait to see what you do with it," Mom said.

"Me either," Dad agreed.

Addie examined both of her parents closely. While this whole scenario was kind of nice, it also felt a little strange. What was up with them? Maybe this was the start of a new relationship.

∞　∞　∞

Over the next few weeks, Addie worked on the buffet in between doctor's appointments, physical therapy, counseling, community service, and rest. It was a bit of a slow process due to her health and lack of strength, but that was okay. Addie could only move so fast for so long. She did enjoy watching the progress she was making through the restoration process. It was satisfying to think she could take something damaged and beat up and make it look like new again.

When she was finally done with it, her parents just stood and stared.

"I can't believe how beautiful you made it look!" Mom said.

"I knew it just needed a little TLC and that you would do it justice." Dad smiled proudly at her for probably the first time since Addie could remember. "Do you want to keep it or sell it?"

"I don't have any use for it," Addie said. "Or a place to keep it in."

"Do you want me to advertise it for you?" Mom seemed like she wanted to have a part in the process, too.

Addie shrugged her shoulders. "If you want." That way she wouldn't have to deal with people.

It only took two days for the buffet to sell. For a thousand dollars.

Addie was in complete shock when Mom handed her the money.

"Not bad for a piece of garbage I found along the side of the road!" Dad said. "Do you want to do more?"

"Maybe?" Did she? Had she found something she could do? While she wasn't ready to admit it out loud, she had found something she enjoyed. Although, she figured her parents already knew that. Even Addie knew there was a smile on her face.

"How about Saturday I hook the trailer up to the truck and we go visit some thrift stores and yard sales? We can make a day of it. We'll see if we can find a few more pieces to keep you busy."

There it was. They wanted to keep her busy. Addie tried to find an argument in her mind about why she couldn't go, but in reality, she wanted to. She wanted to keep busy. The busyness seemed to keep the dreams at bay, at least for a while. They were definitely lessening in frequency. When she was alone in her room at night, she had even been researching ideas for how to make old things look new again, and she had saved a lot of those ideas.

"Okay."

Saturday ended up being a beautiful day. Addie found it refreshing to be out of the house. She also found it refreshing to have her parents' attention. Good attention. Something she had waited so long to receive. Her favorite find of the day was a bench that her dad tried to discourage her from picking out of someone's garbage along the side of the road. This bench was in more than rough shape. Some of the spindles were missing on the back, and one of the legs was broken beyond repair, at least to someone else's eye. But Addie envisioned what it could be.

Dad finally relented, and they got out of the truck to put it in the back with the few other pieces she had purchased.

"Ow!" Addie pulled back her hand.

"What's the matter?" Dad asked.

"A sliver."

"You sure you still want this? It's not too late to dump it back in the garbage pile."

"I want it." Addie said nothing more about the splinter. She didn't even try to pull it out in the truck where Dad might see her. For once in her life, she didn't want to start an argument. It had been a good day. One Addie desperately needed. And she didn't want to ruin it for anything.

Chapter Nineteen

*C*arrie cradled the brooch in her hand as if it were worth a million dollars. Addie just sat back in the corner and sneered. Once again, Grandma Hazel overlooked Addie for Carrie. It was no secret that Carrie was Grandma Hazel's favorite; even Mom alluded to it from time to time. Addie had once heard Mom tell Grandma, "We have another daughter, you know."

Mom must not have realized Addie was close enough to hear it; otherwise, she probably would not have said it at all.

Apparently, Grandma thought Carrie was the perfect child. At least that's how Addie thought Grandma felt. Grandma Hazel was always doing special things for and with Carrie. On this day, Grandma gave Carrie a brooch that had been in the family for some time.

"It used to belong to my grandmother. It's an heirloom that I hope you'll take care of and treasure forever."

What did Addie get?

Nothing.

Zip.

Zilch.

Nada.

Carrie did exactly as Grandma had said, and she took care of that brooch. She even spent her own money on a safe of sorts where she could lock it away and put it on the shelf in the closet.

"What's the point of having something so special if you're never going to use it or even look at it?" As usual, Addie was trying to down play her feelings.

"I don't want to lose it or break it. I might pull it out and wear it for something special or a big event. Maybe my wedding." The look on Carrie's face was one of pure joy. She was simply content knowing she had something that was so extraordinary.

One day, not too far in the future from that time, Addie wanted to get back at Carrie for something silly. Addie had found where Carrie kept the key to her safe, and when Carrie wasn't home, Addie pulled it out and relocated the brooch. She had found a secret cubbyhole that was the perfect hiding place for something so small. No one would ever find it, not even Mom when she was on one of her cleaning sprees.

It took a few years for Carrie to actually notice the brooch was missing. Addie remembered that day well.

"Addie!" Carrie had shouted throughout the house.

"What's your problem?" Addie was clueless at that moment.

Carrie held up the empty box. "Where is it?"

"Where is what?"

"My brooch that Grandma gave me."

At this statement, Addie figured out the issue, but honestly, she could not remember where she had stashed it away. "I have no idea." She wasn't really lying.

"I know you took it!"

"Why would I take it?"

"Where is it?"

"I don't know where it is!" Carrie was loud, but Addie was louder. "You keep it locked up in that box. I don't know where you keep the key."

Carrie glowered at Addie. "I know you took it."

Addie held her hands up in the air as if to concede. "You can look through all my things. You won't find it. I don't know where it is."

Carrie did exactly that. She searched through all of Addie's belongings, through every drawer, through every hiding place Carrie knew of. Addie didn't have any doubts Carrie wouldn't find it, but in some ways, Addie wished she would because that would solve the mystery in her own mind. Where did she put that brooch?

Addie woke up with tears streaming down her face. She lay there for a few moments, trying to recall the details of the dream. It didn't take much effort. She sat up, and after drying her tears, Addie let out a deep sigh. She was feeling pains she had never felt before. And they weren't the physical pains that had become familiar to her in the last several months. These were new feelings. Was it love for her sister? Was it guilt? Did she regret some of the things she had done? Some of the ways she had treated her sister, who had never intentionally hurt anyone or anything in her entire life?

Addie's eyes drifted to the corner of the room where her bed used to be. Immediately, she got up and carefully moved the dresser that now stood in that corner. It was painful and probably not something she should have done by herself, but she had to. Peeling back a little bit of the carpet, she found the long ago forgotten hiding spot. A loose floorboard easily came up, and down in the shadows was a lumpy, worn-out sock. Addie picked it up and knew she had found a treasure. She held it to her chest, crying and repeating over and over again, "I'm sorry, Carrie. I'm sorry. I'm sorry."

Sitting back on the bed, Addie emptied the sock. Still in the perfect condition it was when she had hidden it there, was the brooch Grandma Hazel had given Carrie all those years ago. For all intents and purposes, it was hers now. Grandma Hazel was gone. Carrie was gone. But Addie didn't feel as if she deserved to keep it. Perhaps she should hand it over to her mother, along with yet another confession.

Then she noticed something else was inside the sock. Picking it up, Addie discovered an envelope. Had she put that inside the sock to help the brooch slide in easier and not get stuck on the threads? No. Looking at it closer, she saw that it had her name on it written in Carrie's hand. Addie pulled out the page that was in the envelope and unfolded it.

God, after I write this, I'm going to put it in a safe hiding place. I have yet to feel the time was right to talk to Addie and ask her to forgive me. I have to trust that You will bring it across her path at exactly the time she needs to read it.

The rest of the letter was for her.

Dear Addie, There is something I've wanted to say to you for a long time. I'm sorry. I'm sorry I wasn't the sister you needed. So many times when I was angry with you, I just wouldn't talk to you because I didn't like you. That was wrong. I needed to forgive and forget. The Bible tells us to forgive seven times seventy.

Addie did the math. That was only 490 times.

Surely, Carrie had forgiven her that many times and more. She continued reading.

I don't know why this was something I could never bring myself to say to your face. Maybe it's because God knew you weren't in the spot you needed to be to hear it and take it to heart. We so often want to work ahead of God's timing because we don't understand what He is doing. This is definitely one of those situations. I don't understand. I want to be your friend. Remember what people used to say to us? Best of friends, worst of enemies? I have always wished we could have been the best of friends. Maybe we can be when we're adults and we've learned to move past our hurts. I want you to forgive me for all the times I treated you poorly and without respect. I love you. Your one and only sister, Carrie.

Carrie was asking her for forgiveness? How long ago had she written this? How long had it been hiding? And she had known about the brooch and left it hidden as well. Suddenly, any pleasure she had previously felt in this theft was gone. Completely gone.

The room suddenly became suffocating. Even though it was still very early in the morning, Addie felt the need to do something. Then she thought about the bench and the other pieces of furniture in the garage. If she worked out there for a little bit, she wouldn't bother anyone with her noise, and the actions would take her mind off her findings. Maybe.

Throwing on her favorite jeans and an oversized sweatshirt, she slipped quietly out of the house and into the garage. The morning air held the promise of humidity even though it was the beginning of fall. Smiling, she walked over to the bench that lay on the worktable, just waiting for her to bring new life into it. It would take a good amount of time, but it was going to be worth it. Addie could already picture it in her mind's eye, and it looked beautiful.

Grabbing some of her dad's tools, she began pulling off all the pieces that were so damaged they needed to be replaced instead of repaired. That included removing three of the six spindles on the back and the shattered leg. Not wanting to get another splinter, Addie grabbed a pair of her dad's work gloves to protect her hands.

All the tugging and pulling made her chest ache some. Knowing it would be easy to overdo it, Addie worked in short spurts throughout the day. By dinnertime, she had all the spindles and the leg replaced. It looked a little bit like a Frankenstein bench, but she knew some sanding and a few coats of paint would do wonders.

A week or so later, for some reason, Carrie's funeral suddenly popped into Addie's mind. Surely there had been one. But Addie had not gone. She was probably still in the hospital at the time, but everyone else was more than likely glad she was not able to attend.

Her mind wandered to what Carrie's funeral must have been like, but then another thought dawned on her. She pulled out her phone and logged into her social media account. She pulled up Carrie's as well. While Addie had never accepted Carrie's invite, Addie knew Carrie kept her account open and public so anyone who wanted to see what she posted could. Addie recalled Carrie saying something about it being a witnessing tool. She often posted Scripture verses, songs, and whatever else she said God laid on her heart. Addie never followed Carrie because Carrie posted the type of things Addie didn't want to see. If she ever wanted to know what Carrie was up to, Addie could always just go and look.

When Carrie's page came up on Addie's phone, she was almost in shock. It seemed as if hundreds of people had posted messages on Carrie's page after her death about how she had helped them through a difficult time or had been a word of encouragement to them in a time of need. People everywhere–there were posts from all over the world–had been touched by Carrie in some way or another. Who knew Carrie had that many contacts?

Addie read through a few of them, but then one caught her attention.

Thanks for streaming Carrie's funeral. She touched me in so many ways even though I never had met her in person. What a touching tribute to someone so special. She lived a short life, but it was one well-lived.

There was a link with this post that Addie clicked on. It was the funeral. She began watching it. There was the usual message from their pastor, but it wasn't until the cameras moved and panned through the crowd that Addie saw how many people had attended. Did their family even know that many people? Were there that many people in their small town?

The sermon was short, reminiscent of Carrie's life, but there was one thing that stuck out to Addie. It was a verse the pastor read.

"'Now listen, you who say, "Today or tomorrow we will go to this or that city, spend a year there, carry on business and make money." Why, you do not even know what will happen tomorrow. What is your life? You are a mist that appears for a little while and then vanishes. Instead, you ought to say, "If it is the Lord's will, we will live and do this or that." As it is, you boast in your arrogant schemes. All such boasting is evil. If anyone, then, knows the good they ought to do and doesn't do it, it is sin for them.' That comes from James 4:13-17. Our life is a vapor. None of us knows how many days we have to live. Making plans for the future isn't a bad thing, but it is today that counts. What are we doing for today? What are we doing today that will make a difference in the kingdom of God? Carrie lived each day to the fullest in that regard. She knew tomorrow wasn't promised. She lived for God every single day.

"Some of you may have known Carrie a little better than I did, but I think we can all agree that she had an aura about her. Her face glowed with the Holy Spirit. Her eyes were always bright, full of life and love. She was always smiling. Her laugh was infectious, and she wasn't afraid to share it."

"Don't forget her perfectly formed teeth." Addie couldn't help but be snarky to the screen face of the pastor. Addie sighed, almost bored with the Scripture and the talk of Carrie, but at the same time intrigued.

Then, to top it all off, the pastor opened up the service for any who wanted to say a word or two or three thousand about Carrie. Many people had much to say. Yes, Carrie was only in her mid-twenties, but she had definitely lived that short life as if each day were her last.

"I needed someone to pray with me in the middle of the night, and Carrie was there," one person was saying.

The microphone was passed to another person.

"It didn't seem to matter how bad of a person I was, Carrie told me that God was always there, knocking at my heart's door, waiting for me to answer. She was right. It's because of her that I am a child of God today."

"Thank you to Carrie's family for postponing the funeral a few days so that her friends in far-away places could come and pay her the appropriate tribute."

Similar stories continued for quite some time. Addie had to fast-forward through them, but she did notice the time at the bottom of the video. Carrie's funeral service lasted for over two hours. With the pastor's message only being about fifteen minutes, that meant that for an hour and forty-five minutes, people were bragging about all Carrie had done for them.

"Seriously!"

Addie was glad she wasn't there. If she had been physically able to go, her parents probably would have forced her to as a form of punishment for taking away their favorite daughter. Then she would have had to sit through all two hours of talking. Not to mention all the hugs people might have tried to give Addie in expressing their condolences. Addie knew those hugs would have all been as fake as the people who gave them.

Addie clicked out of the video and tossed her phone down on the bed. Even in death, Carrie out-did her. Addie figured that when she died, no one would care.

She'd be lucky to get a funeral, let alone have anyone show up besides her parents. Even then, her parents would only come because they felt obligated. She was their daughter, after all.

For the rest of the day, as much as she tried, Addie could not get the pictures and the voices from the funeral out of her mind. It was disturbing. It made her think about what mark she would leave on the world. Would she leave any? Was that something people actually aspired to?

Hoping the noise of the sander and the concentration it took to refinish the bench would drown out the funeral replaying in her mind and the thoughts it made her think, she went out to the garage and got to work. But nothing could make her mind shut up.

It was the shouting match heard round the world, or at least around their small community. Addie had never liked small-town living where everyone not only knew everyone else but knew everyone else's business as well. It probably didn't help that Addie and her father had the shouting match in the front yard, either. More than likely, all fifteen hundred-ish members of the community heard it.

"You're not leaving!" Dad followed her as she banged

toward the front door, suitcase in hand.

"Oh, yes, I am!" If Addie had taken the time to look back, she would have seen the suitcase get stuck on the door frame, almost yanking her arm out of the socket and giving her excruciating pain in the shoulder. This gave her dad the couple of seconds he needed to grab her arm and try to drag her back into the house.

In spite of the pain she knew it would cause, Addie pulled her arm as hard as she could to remove it from her father's grip. Leaving the suitcase caught on the doorjamb, she ran out the front door.

"I don't need those clothes anyway. Brad will buy me knew ones."

"You are not leaving!" Dad repeated himself.

"Oh, yes, I am!" Addie repeated herself.

"First of all, you have no idea what kind of person this Brad is. I've heard stories, and none of them are good. Sanders told me Brad has been arrested several times."

"I don't care what Officer Sanders has to say. Brad said that he was falsely accused and the police have it out for him. I'm choosing to believe him. I personally know how Officer Sanders can be." Addie spit out the police officer's name with hatred.

Dad looked a little stunned. "You'd listen to a boy you just met over your parents?"

"He's not a boy. He's a man, and he loves me."

"Not anywhere near as much as your mother and I love you."

"You have a funny way of showing it!"

Dad paused in the argument and sighed. "Can we please take this inside and talk rationally?"

Addie was torn. She wanted to leave, but she also needed her suitcase that was still stuck in the door. At least she thought it was. Glancing that way, she noticed it was unstuck and no longer visible. Anger rose a level higher in her. With her chest heaving, she ran into the house. "Who touched my suitcase?" she hollered.

"I put it back in your room." Mom was standing there with her arms akimbo. The look on her face dared Addie to go get it.

Addie decided against it, thinking they would probably slam and lock the door once she went inside to retrieve the baggage.

By this time, Dad had come in and closed the front door. There was no point in trying to escape this place her parents called a home. Flopping on the couch, Addie crossed her arms over her chest, just waiting for her parents to drop the bomb.

"You are grounded. You aren't going anywhere, not even to school since we can't trust that you'll come home." Dad wasn't pulling any punches this time.

"That's not fair!" Addie stood to her feet and shouted.

"It doesn't have to be."

Addie seared both her parents with a look that could kill before she stomped off to her bedroom and slammed the door.

Coming out of this dream of what really was, Addie knew her parents had been right; although she wasn't ready to fully admit that. Brad was not the guy he portrayed himself to be to Addie. It wasn't long before he found himself in prison for a nice, long visit. He had only used Addie for what he wanted, just like everyone else did.

Chapter Twenty

om walked into the room and suddenly stopped. "Do you want to get up and shower? I can help you."

Addie didn't really feel like getting a shower, although she knew she probably smelled bad. She knew that before her mom walked into the room and sniffed. Addie could smell herself, and it wasn't good.

"I can change the sheets while you're up. I know I enjoy getting into a clean bed after not feeling well. Do you need help in the bathroom?" Not waiting for Addie to reply about whether she wanted a shower or not, Mom began pulling some clean pajamas out of Addie's drawers.

"I'll be fine. The accident was months ago." Addie didn't want help from anyone. Still having to stay at her parents' house was bad enough. She couldn't find a job or money to buy a car to get her to one. Selling the furniture was helping, but she was setting that money aside for an apartment.

"Well, leave the door unlocked just in case you need

me." Then Mom went to the linen closet to pull out some fresh sheets.

"I won't need you." Addie scooched to the edge of the bed and then stood up slowly. Dizziness still came and found her from time to time, and she certainly didn't want her mom to think she needed help. How embarrassing would that be? Addie picked up the clothes Mom had set next to her on the bed and headed for the bathroom. A clean bath towel sat on the edge of the sink, waiting for her. Turning on the water to let it run for a moment while she undressed, Addie found herself moving slower than she ever had before. Showers usually took only a couple of minutes from start to finish. But the scalding hot water sure did feel good on her back. Not so much on the front of her chest where most of her incision scar still remained even though she had taken the nurse's advice and used vitamin E on it daily. She basked in the warmth until the warmth ran out. Slowly, she dried off and got dressed. Clean clothes felt amazing, too.

When she returned to the bedroom, she noticed a candle burning. It was lavender, her favorite.

At Mom's voice, Addie turned around. "I lit a candle in there for you. I know lavender is your favorite. I thought it might help you relax."

Relax? That's all she'd been doing for the past several months. She thought after six months, life would be back to normal, but nothing was. But she did find the candle was calming to her anxious soul.

"Thanks," was all she said.

When she walked fully back into the bedroom, Addie also noticed Mom had put a clean quilt on the bed. The quilt Carrie had given her for Christmas. She had wondered what happened to that quilt. Addie didn't take it with her when she moved out. Perhaps Carrie noticed and took it with her to the other side of the country, seeing as Addie didn't appreciate the gift anyway. Maybe it had been in one of the boxes stacked in the bedroom. Or, it could have been her mom. Saving an abandoned quilt that Carried had made with love was definitely something Mom would have done. It annoyed Addie that her mom would pull it out now. What was she trying to say? Surprisingly, Mom didn't mention what Carrie had told Addie that Christmas morning. *"I prayed for you with every stitch."*

With that memory, Addie wasn't sure how she felt about that quilt being on the bed. Yes, she did. She didn't like it at all. Pulling back the blankets, she carefully settled into bed. Expending as much energy as it did to shower and change her clothes still exhausted her. And as much as she didn't want to admit it, her mom was right; a clean body, clean clothes, and clean bedding felt wonderful. But the last few days she took to have a pity party were worth it.

Addie lay back and closed her eyes to rest for a few moments, but something was unsettling. Her legs were burning. Throwing back the covers, she felt relief. The edges of the quilt toward the bottom of the bed peeked out at her. It wasn't her body temperature that bothered her; it was that quilt. It was like Carrie's presence was in the room with her.

Addie's heart rate increased as she thought about her sister. Her dead sister. The sister she killed. Looking around the darkening room, Addie fully expected to see an apparition appear. Finally, she was able to get her breathing and heartbeats back to a more normal rate.

"This is ridiculous!" she scolded herself. "There are no such things as ghosts."

Still, there was the quilt, and Addie wanted to be as far away from it as she could. Yanking it off the bed, she tossed it over the chair in the far corner of the room. She would be sleeping without it.

Between showering, changing, and fighting with the heavy quilt, Addie was spent. Leaning all the way back in bed, she closed her eyes to try and sleep.

But the dreams wouldn't let her.

Running. Addie was running. From what she didn't know. She was dressed in a nightgown, and her bare feet splashed in cold mud puddles that filled potholes along a deserted street. As she glanced back, she knew someone was behind her, following her, not chasing per se but definitely

following. Addie didn't know who he was, but somehow she recognized it as a man. He had something she needed, but for some reason, she was afraid of him and didn't want what he was offering. No matter where she turned, he was there, always waiting, reaching out his arms to her.

As soon as she saw the alley to her right, she ran down it, hoping to stop running and be able to catch her breath. Seeing a door, she opened it and found a room where she could hide. She closed the door as quickly and quietly as she could. Addie held her breath in an effort to be completely silent but then came the knocking. The knocking didn't stop. It wasn't panicked knocking like someone needed help, it was a more patient knocking like the man knew she was there, and he was going to keep on knocking until she opened the door.

While Addie dreamed, she tossed and turned and shivered. She may have been dreaming, but she was conscious of what was going on around her at the same time. All the remaining blankets were off the bed now. Her dad came in and just stood staring at her for a few moments. She wanted to reach out to him and have him save her from whoever was chasing her, but she couldn't move outside of her dream. Finally, he picked up the blankets and covered her. He pulled the quilt Carrie had made off the chair and covered Addie with that one as well. He walked toward the doorway and seemed about to leave the room when he stopped suddenly. In one smooth motion, he was kneeling on the floor next to the bed, praying for his daughter.

"Lord, I don't know what Addie is experiencing in her dreams, but I can tell she's distressed. She's struggling. She has run away from You for so long. Help heal her body and her heart. Help her to look to You and see that You are all she needs. Give me the words to say to her. Use me, even if I don't realize You're using me. I'd rather that be the case anyway. I have a tendency to preach or holler at her using my own words. It's no wonder she doesn't listen to me. I want her to see You. I want her to hear You. Be with her, Lord. Calm her anxious spirit. Bind the enemy so she won't be fearful.

"'But now, this is what the Lord says—he who created you, Jacob, he who formed you, Israel: "Do not fear, for I have redeemed you; I have summoned you by name; you are mine."' (Isaiah 43:1)

"'So do not fear, for I am with you; do not be dismayed, for I am your God. I will strengthen you and help you; I will uphold you with my righteous right hand.' (Isaiah 41:10)

"'Say to those with fearful hearts, "Be strong, do

not fear; your God will come, he will come with vengeance; with divine retribution he will come to save you.' (Isaiah 35:4)

"'He will cover you with his feathers, and under his wings you will find refuge; his faithfulness will be your shield and rampart. You will not fear the terror of night, nor the arrow that flies by day.' (Psalm 91:4-5)

"'Do not be afraid of them; the LORD your God himself will fight for you.' (Deuteronomy 3:22)

"'Though an army besiege me, my heart will not fear; though war break out against me, even then I will be confident.' (Psalm 27:3)

"'So don't be afraid; you are worth more than many sparrows.'" (Matthew 10:31)

He prayed and quoted Scripture until her body no longer thrashed.

∞ ∞ ∞

In her nightmare, all of a sudden, Addie felt a warmth come over her. She didn't know what it was. There was still the knocking at the door, as persistent and patient as ever, but something around her changed. She wasn't scared. It was like someone had wrapped their arms around her and was holding her, shielding her from anything or anyone that might want to hurt her. An unknown peace came over her. Although it took a while, rest finally came.

Chapter Twenty-One

"*If you don't have a relationship with Christ, you can't expect any human relationship to be successful.*"

Addie abruptly awoke from her dreams...memories...nightmares. Whatever they were. Carrie's voice was reverberating in her head. This particular quote of Carrie's was from a conversation they'd had after Addie came home from another failed date. Addie didn't want to hear it then, and she certainly didn't want to relive that moment, or any of her disastrous dating moments from her teen years, or her adult years, for that matter. She had been, and still was, a hot mess, and she knew it. Everyone knew it. Not a whole lot had changed. That was obvious by the number of so-called friends who had called her since the accident. No one knew she was in an accident. And apparently, no one cared or missed her at all.

Lying there in the dark, Addie began to rethink some of her relationships. Carrie was still best friends with her first best friend who she met in first grade, Eileen.

Or at least she had been until ...

Addie shook her head a little in an effort to erase that thought.

Carrie loved to tell the story of their first day of first grade. Carrie had painstakingly chosen her outfit for the first day. When she came into the classroom, the teacher told her to sit at the empty desk. The girl sitting next to Carrie was just about as sweet as Carrie and was wearing the same outfit. It was the beginning of a life-long friendship.

Addie didn't have any stories like that.

Truly, Carrie was a loyal friend. Friends didn't come and go in her life. They came and stayed. The list of her friends grew while the list of people Addie offended in one way or another grew, but the friends on her list were fewer and fewer. Maybe she was down to none. Addie could hardly remember any of her early classmates. No one probably remembered her either. Or if they did remember her, it probably wasn't with good memories. It was those memories that came to her mind now.

There was Heidi, who started out being Addie's friend, but then one day all Heidi wanted to do was pick a fight. Addie truly had no idea what went wrong in that friendship. Heidi had made new friends and gotten weird. That wasn't Addie's fault!

Then there was Katie. She and Addie had started out as friends. One day, Addie thought it would be funny to play a joke on Katie and put super glue on her chair.

When Katie got back up after sitting, the fabric of her skirt had torn enough that she had to go to the office and call her mom to bring her something else to wear. She didn't speak to Addie ever again. It was a joke. Apparently, Katie couldn't take a joke.

As she got older and boys were part of her tiny circle of friends, they didn't stay long either. Mark was interested in her until he found out she was calling Daniel on a regular basis. Addie figured it was better that he was gone because if he was going to be jealous of every boy she talked to, he wasn't worth having around.

A thought came to Addie. The other day when she was sorting through a box of Carrie's books looking for something to read, she remembered tossing aside an old elementary school yearbook. After tossing aside all the Christian fiction and devotionals Carrie had, Addie found nothing interesting to read. But now, that yearbook might be fascinating. Addie pulled out the pile of books she had put back into the box until she found the yearbook at the bottom. Snuggling under the blankets on her bed, she settled in with a smirk, expecting to bring up some good memories. "Good memories" being subjective, of course.

Quickly turning the pages to get to her class photograph, memories immediately started flooding Addie's mind.

There was Kaylee who Addie hit it off with right away. They thought they would be best friends until her father's job transferred the family to another state.

Jessica would have been a good friend, too, if it wasn't for her mom. Addie had gone over once to spend the night and brought nail polish with her. That evening, Jessica's mom had come into the room and asked what the smell was.

"What smell?" asked Jessica.

When her mom saw the nail polish, she flipped out.

"You lied to me, Jessica!"

Addie remembered crying as she heard Jessica's mom spanking her with a belt in another room. She never understood it. Jessica had not lied to her mom. Addie was never invited back to spend the night after Jessica changed schools. The two of them never saw each other again. That was probably exactly what Jessica's mom had been planning.

Addie saw a picture of Lila next. Addie went over to her house one time, too. While there, Lila's parents had left the kids home alone. Lila and Addie had been playing outside near the doghouse. When they got tired of whatever game they were playing, they got up to do something else. As they started to run away, Lila's dog grabbed a hold of Addie by the thigh and wouldn't let go. That resulted in a huge bruise for Addie and a dead pet for Lila. Lila didn't speak to Addie after that, except to tell her it was her fault for having to put down their dog. If Addie had not tried to run to the house, the dog wouldn't have bit her. Like most things, Addie didn't think it was her fault.

Kevin. How could she forget about Kevin? He was the boy Addie was planning her wedding around in fourth grade. Addie dreamed of being the perfect wife and keeping her house clean for Kevin. At least until Kevin's pastor father said Addie wasn't good enough for his boy. Addie snorted as she thought about it. Did Kevin's dad really think their relationship was going to last past the fourth grade? Was he really that concerned about an impending wedding that he had to alienate Kevin from her? Yup. She was that intimidating, even in elementary school.

What about Ellen? Oh, wait. No. Addie couldn't consider Ellen a lost friend. Addie never had a kind word for her. Kind words were all Carrie's thing. Ellen was the overweight girl Addie made fun of on the bus to and from swimming lessons each summer. Why? Addie didn't know. Ellen was an easy target, and Addie took advantage of that.

If she had them, Addie could have gone through all of her old yearbooks and told stories of why each classmate was not her friend. No one liked her; no one wanted to be her friend. But Carrie. Now Carrie was a completely different story.

Addie closed the yearbook and tossed it back in the box. The trip down memory lane had not been what she thought it might be. There were no good memories of childhood friends. Addie had no good memories of anything at all.

Chapter Twenty-Two

"There's a Ladies' Fellowship meeting at church tonight. Do you want to go?"

It was all Addie could do not to snort. Did her mother truly think she wanted to go? "No thanks," she squeaked out, restraining herself from saying something beyond rude.

"I think you would enjoy it. It will be good for you to get out for a little bit. You've only gone out for your doctor's appointments for the past several months. And those are even fewer and farther between now. "

"I don't think so." Addie tilted her head and squinted her eyes in argument.

"What if I said you had to go?"

"You can't make me."

"Oh, I think I can. You never want to go to church with us. This is different. There's no sermon. There's no singing. It's just ladies getting together for fellowship and refreshment."

Addie was tired of the back and forth. She was tired of her parents harping on her to go to church. Maybe if she went to this one thing, they would stop pestering her. It wouldn't be too long until she was able to go back to work and get out on her own again. That was a day she looked forward to!

"Fine!"

Mom smiled as if she had won a huge victory. "Be ready at 6:30."

Addie responded by letting out a huge sigh. "You owe me for this."

"I gave you life."

With no more snarky responses, Addie left to go shower and get ready for this shindig that was sure to be a good time. Sarcastic thoughts were just oozing out of her.

In an effort to show her distaste for going, Addie decided to skip the shower. She threw on any old clothes she knew her mom would find not appropriate for church. In fact, she wore yoga pants and a baggy sweatshirt that hung off one of her shoulders. It was one of her favorite and most comfortable outfits, yet she had never worn it outside of the house.

As she came back into the kitchen when it was time to leave, Mom didn't act like she even noticed.

"Are you ready to go?" was all she asked, with barely a look in Addie's direction.

"As ready as I'll ever be."

"I think it will do you good to get out of the house. You've been cooped up far too long."

"Tell me about it."

"You girls have fun." Dad suddenly appeared out of nowhere, causing Addie to jump slightly.

"We will."

A look passed between the two of them. Addie caught it. She had no idea what it meant, but she knew they were up to something. Addie had a feeling she was going to regret this night.

Slumping down in the passenger seat of the car, propping her elbow on the edge of the door, and resting her head on her hand, Addie was so not looking forward to this. When they first arrived, no one really paid much attention to her. She was fine with that. That meant she didn't have to speak to anyone. While her mom was greeting some of the other ladies, Addie helped herself to the refreshment table.

"Is this your first time here, too?"

A woman, who didn't look to be too much older than Addie, sidled up to her at the refreshment table.

"Yup." Addie was in no mood for talking. It was bad enough her mom made her set foot in church. Making friends was not on her agenda. Obviously, the friend thing never worked out for her anyway.

"Me too. I'm Courtney."

"Addie. Hi." Addie kept her words as short as possible to hopefully discourage Courtney from continuing the conversation. Courtney looked like the type of person Carrie would have been best friends with. Courtney even looked like Carrie, the perky cheerleader type. Perfect. Addie couldn't help but raise one corner of her lip in a sneer as she poured herself a cup of coffee.

Fortunately, a little bell ringing caught everyone's attention.

"It's time we got started, ladies. If everyone would take their seats we can begin with prayer requests."

Addie rolled her eyes but quietly took her plate of snacks and cup of coffee and went to sit in the last row of chairs. Mom came and sat beside her, patting Addie on the knee.

After everyone ran out of prayer requests to share, they prayed as a group. Different ladies took turns praying, depending on who felt led. It seemed to take forever, and Addie kept looking at her watch to see how long each one prayed. It became a game that kept her from falling asleep. How did they expect people to close their eyes and be quiet and still for so long without taking a nap?

Eventually, the prayers ended. The lady who had rung the bell walked to the front of the room and stood behind a small podium.

I thought there wasn't going to be any preaching, Addie wondered to herself.

"I have a very special guest for us tonight. You all know I have been asking for prayers for my niece for some time now. Well, God answered those prayers way beyond anything I could have imagined. God brought her back from a life of self-destruction and put her on a road where she is willing to share her story with whomever she meets." The woman held out her hand, palm up, toward someone in the front row. "Courtney."

Oh, brother!

The two women shared a long hug.

Courtney situated herself behind the podium and shuffled a couple of papers around. "Let me see, where do I want to begin? There are so many things I want to tell you, but I have to condense my story, or else we will be here until next week. I wrote down the most important things to help keep me on track."

She took a deep breath and blew it out through pursed lips before continuing. "My story is hard to tell. Not because I don't want you to hear it, but because I can't believe I lived it. I don't know what I was thinking. To start at the beginning a little bit, I grew up in a Christian home with loving parents. They were an example of godliness to me, but for the most part, I ignored them. I thought what I wanted was better. My way of life was more fun than the stuffy, religious one they lived."

Addie was beginning to see why her mother wanted her here tonight, and she didn't appreciate being deceived. Mom knew of this girl's testimony and wanted to shove it in Addie's face. Folding her arms across her chest and slouching in her chair, Addie resigned herself to the fact she was stuck for the time being, but that didn't mean she had to listen.

"Maybe my parents didn't give me everything I wanted, but that was no excuse for the way I behaved or for the way I treated them," Courtney went on. "All the choices I made were my own, and most of them were bad ones. I was hateful to everyone. I used to wonder why I didn't have any friends, but now, looking back, it's a wonder I didn't have more enemies than I did. Anything you can think of, I did it. Alcohol, drugs, sex, abortion, and more. There probably isn't any bad thing you can think of that I didn't do. And I didn't care who I hurt along the way.

"What I did have was people who prayed for me. My parents were on their knees for me daily. I know now that all of you were praying for me as well, someone you didn't even know. Some spoiled kid who was reaping the consequences of her decisions. I want you to know that your prayers are why I am here today. Although I didn't know what it was at the time, I could definitely feel a pull on my heart. Something, or Someone, was calling out to me. Believe me when I say I tried to ignore it. I had no intentions of changing my lifestyle. I was happy the way I was. At least that's what I thought."

For some reason, Addie couldn't help but hear some of what Courtney was saying, even though she tried to tune the voice out. Courtney's words resonated within Addie. The two of them were so much alike. Perhaps they could have been friends if Courtney hadn't turned her life around and was now going to church and preaching.

"Then one day, I couldn't take it anymore. The Voice calling out to me was too strong. I couldn't resist it any longer, and I wasn't sure I wanted to. One day, while I was by myself, in my bedroom, with the intentions of setting up a date with a new guy, I found myself texting him I was busy and couldn't come. It was strange. I didn't know what had come over me. At least in that moment I didn't. I found out later that my aunt," Courtney looked lovingly at her aunt on the front row who was sopping up her tears with a tissue, "had organized a prayer group where the ladies had a specific time each day to pray for me."

The words "for me" came out in more of a whisper, as if Courtney was trying to hold in the tears. She pointed to her chest and then pointed to the ladies who were listening. "You prayed for me." She pointed at a different person each time she said the words. "You prayed for me. You prayed for me.

"At that moment, a verse kept rattling around in my head. I'm not even sure where I originally heard it. I'm sure it was from my parents or maybe something from an old Sunday school class I had been in, but I know I never memorized it. James 4:7, 'Submit yourselves, then, to God. Resist the devil, and he will flee from you.' Believe it or not, I wanted the devil to flee. I didn't want him tempting me anymore. At that moment, I had to give everything up. I had to give up the men in my life who were there for one purpose only. They gave me the moment of attention I thought I so desired. I gave them the pleasure they were seeking without having a true and loving relationship. I went into my kitchen and poured out every bit of beer and wine I had in my apartment. I deleted most of the contacts on my phone. I threw away a closet full of inappropriate clothes. If I was going to change, I knew it needed to be immediate and complete. There was no going back.

"After expending an enormous amount of energy doing all of that, I fell down on my knees. I knew about prayer and God because my parents had taken me to church since I was three days old. I knew what to say. I knew what God expected of me. I knew He didn't want anything except my heart and my love. I knew He would help me clear out all the detrimental things in my life. That was the day I asked Christ to be a part of my life. No more playing games. No more running. No more trying to hide when I knew I couldn't anyway."

Courtney stopped to take a sip of water and wipe her face. Tears had been running down her cheeks constantly, yet her voice remained strong.

"You prayed for me. While you were on your knees as a group praying for me, I was on my knees fighting the battle of a lifetime. I couldn't have won that battle if it wasn't for each of you. I want to thank you for that. Without you, I would not be here today. Who knows where I would be and what I would be doing. Who knows if I would even still be alive. I certainly have no idea. But I am sure of two things and those are Christ's love for His children and the power of prayer. I am living proof."

Addie hadn't realized it, but tears had been coursing down her cheeks as well. Was it just the fact that she was in a roomful of crying women? Was she hormonal? No. Even she had to admit it was more than that. Mom handed her a tissue and then put her arm around Addie's shoulders. Addie didn't shrug her off, at least not right away. She did find it a little uncomfortable to be that physically close to her mom since it had never been a part of their relationship. In some ways, though, it felt good.

"I needed Someone who would love me for who and what I was. I needed Someone to understand me. Someone was there. It was God. He was where He had always been, just waiting for me. He had been patiently knocking on the door of my heart. And ... "

Then Courtney stepped from behind the podium to grab something. She unfolded it and held it up. "This is a quilt my aunt gave me after I accepted Christ. She gave it to me with a note that said God could take all the ugly pieces of my life and weave them into something beautiful. If you look closely at this quilt and at each fabric by itself, you will see there are some really ugly ones."

People laughed at that.

"But when sewn together with other fabrics and you look at it as a whole, it is a beautiful work of art. And that's what we are when we are in Christ. He wants to take our ugly pasts and use them for His glory. That's when they become beautiful."

Addie couldn't imagine anything in her past becoming beautiful. She had been like her own artwork in her parents' eyes: ugly.

After tossing and turning for a couple of hours, Addie threw back the covers and got out of bed. Maybe some cool air would help clear her mind. Quietly, she crept down the stairs and opened the sliding glass door to the back deck.

"Can't sleep either?"

Addie jumped and closed the door a little harder than she planned.

"I didn't mean to startle you."

If Addie had known the deck was already occupied, she would've chosen somewhere else to get fresh air.

"What's keeping you up?" Dad asked

Addie shrugged her shoulders. "I don't know." But she did know. Everything Courtney had said earlier that evening reverberated through her head. Her mind wouldn't stop spinning in circles.

"I have a lot on my mind, too. I wasn't always the perfect guy you see before you today."

Addie knew her dad was trying to lighten the mood, but it wasn't working. She didn't find him funny.

"Have a seat." He gestured to the Adirondack chair that tilted toward him but also allowed them both to look out onto the yard. She obliged. The air was cool enough for Addie to wrap herself up in a blanket that hung on the back of the chair. The air held a hint of the smell of coming rain and dead autumn foliage.

He sighed before he continued speaking. "I'm sorry I was so hard on you while you were growing up."

Addie shrugged her shoulders. She didn't care. Or

did she?

"I just saw a lot of me in you and didn't want to admit it."

Now Addie's ears perked up a little bit. She looked at him and caught his eye in the pale moonlight, waiting for him to continue.

"I caused a lot of trouble in my day. I gave my parents grief probably every waking moment of my teenage years. I know they weren't upset or sad the day I moved out of the house. My mom even asked if I needed help packing. She said it nicely, but I knew what was really on her heart."

Here, he paused and took a deep breath. "I never wanted it to be that way with you, even though I saw that was where your life was headed."

Addie inwardly rolled her eyes. *So he was glad when I moved out.*

"I was not exactly sad the day you decided to leave home. I shouldn't have been that way and have asked God to forgive me over and over again. But I never asked you to forgive me. I never asked you to forgive me all the times when I was frustrated with your behavior and had to walk away before I lost it and did something I'd regret. Little did I know the walking away was what I would come to regret. You needed me to be your dad, and I bailed."

Addie looked him in the eyes. *An apology? Someone was apologizing to her?* She didn't know what to say, so she kept silent.

Dad looked down at his slippers and shook his head. "I did some bad things when I was a teenager."

So the apple doesn't fall far from the tree. Maybe this had been Grandma Hazel's aversion to her.

"There were nights I heard my mom cry herself to sleep. I heard and didn't care."

Addie could definitely relate to that.

"I was always in trouble at school. My grades were horrible. I was headed nowhere fast. I think I was suspended more than I was in school. Did you know I failed two grades because of absences due to suspension?"

"No." Addie decided she could speak one word. Maybe they had more in common than she ever suspected.

"I cheated on exams. I was always interrupting the class. I started fights on a weekly basis."

Addie didn't think that sounded so bad.

"And then there was the time I punched a teacher in the mouth."

Okay. Maybe that did.

"That was the last straw for the school. They kicked me out permanently, and I ended up getting my GED. My parents said that since I was done with school, I needed to be out on my own. They were tired of trying to form me into a responsible member of society."

At his pause, he looked up and met Addie's eyes.

"And then I met your mother." The smile on his face said it all. "She invited me to church. She didn't ask me to change who I was, but she made me want to change. I accepted Christ as my Savior and turned my life around. It wasn't until I realized I had a problem that I could or even wanted to change. But the Lord helped me with that. You can change too if you want. You can come to Christ any time. He is standing at the door of your heart, knocking, waiting for you to answer."

There was that knocking on the door again. Addie had dreamed someone was knocking on the door, Courtney had mentioned it, and now her dad said the same thing. Is that what was happening in her dreams/nightmares? Was God chasing after her?

"I really wanted your life to be different than mine, but you are so much like me. I know you can't learn from the mistakes of others. You're going to have to learn by making mistakes all on your own. I know because I had the same thick head and hard heart. Maybe someday you'll find someone who wants to make you change."

Dad was silent for a few moments before getting up. "I'm going to try and get some sleep now. Maybe God woke me because he wanted me to have this chat with you."

He patted Addie on the knee before leaving her alone on the deck. In spite of the darkness, Addie was certain she had seen the glittering of tears in his eyes.

In the days following the Ladies Fellowship meeting and Dad's chat, Addie spent a lot of time in thought. More time than she had ever spent thinking before. Carrie came to her mind. Often. While many Christians Addie had known through the years were somewhat fake, Carrie never was. What one saw with Carrie was who Carrie was. She didn't pretend to be one person with one crowd and a different person with another. She was constant. She was always the same.

"Jesus Christ is the same yesterday, today and forever."

That was a verse Addie remembered Carrie quoting one time when she was going through something difficult. Carrie would often just take a deep breath and whisper that verse over and over again as if she were praying it. Carrie not only talked the talk, she walked the walk. She was an example of Christ-like living to all who knew her.

Including Addie.

And that gave her an idea.

Addie walked down to the kitchen, where her mom was fixing dinner. "Mom, would you mind if I used your car? I just wanted to go to the store to grab something."

Mom studied her for a moment. She must have seen something different in Addie because she just said, "I would be happy to drive you anywhere you want to go. Don't forget, you still are not allowed to drive yet."

Addie hadn't forgotten about that, but she hoped her mom had. She started to walk back up to her room.

"Are you sure I can't take you somewhere? I don't have to go into the store with you. I'll wait in the car."

Addie thought about that. It was probably the best life was going to get for a while. Turning back around to face her mom, she said, "I just wanted to stop at the bookstore."

Mom bobbed her head back and forth. "That is not a problem at all. Let me just go run a brush through my hair and put on some shoes."

"Thanks."

"It's my pleasure."

As Mom walked past Addie to go upstairs, she gently put her hand on Addie's cheek. It almost tore Addie apart. The gentle touch. The scent of her mom's hand that forever smelled like a mixture of garlic and dish soap. It was a pleasant aroma, one that seemed to be uniquely her mom. Why had she never thought about that before?

That was the first real conversation she and her mom had had in Addie didn't know how long. It was ... nice.

At the bookstore, it didn't take Addie long to find what she was looking for. There was a display right at the front near the registers. She picked out a blank journal and took it up to the register.

"Hey, Addie! You're looking very well." Mrs. Schwartz used to be the librarian at the school. Carrie knew her much better than Addie did since she spent much more time in the library, but Addie definitely knew who Mrs. Schwartz was.

Addie's mood suddenly changed, and she was not in the mood for conversation. "I'm fine. How much do I owe you?" She really just wanted to pay for her journal and get out of there before she saw someone else she knew.

"That's $15 even."

Addie swiped her card, hoping to not have to talk anymore.

Mrs. Schwartz must have taken the hint because all she said was, "Tell your mom that all is well."

Addie didn't respond to the comment. Instead, she grabbed her bag and headed out the door as fast as she could. Small-town living! One could never escape being seen. Addie took a few deep breaths to calm herself. There had been a change coming over her earlier in the day and she didn't want to spoil that feeling just because someone spoke to her.

"Thanks, Mom," she said again as they drove home.

"You okay?" Mom asked.

"Yeah." Addie did not want to share what she was feeling. She was a

little confused about them herself.

"What did you get?"

Addie held up the book. "I got a blank journal. I thought I'd take some lessons from Carrie and write things down. I feel like there's so much going on in my head that I'm drowning. Maybe if I can organize my thoughts, it will help."

Mom smiled. "I'm always here if you ever need anything."

Addie smiled back. "I know." And she did know. Mom and Dad had always been available, but Addie had never taken them up on their offers to talk about anything ... ever.

"I'll be in my room if you need me."

"Okay."

In the quiet and alone of the room where she and Carrie had shared their childhood, Addie got comfortable on the bed and placed the journal on her lap. She caressed the cover, thinking about Carrie and all the journals she'd kept over the years. After that one day, Addie had not touched any of them again. It felt like an invasion of Carrie's privacy, even though Carrie was gone, and even though invading Carrie's privacy had never bothered Addie before.

What was the matter with her?

With pen in hand, Addie started writing down her jumbled thoughts. At first, every sentence was random. Nothing made sense. But the more she wrote, the better she felt. It was a release. Writing things down released some of the anger and sadness that were so much a part of her life.

She looked up from her scribblings for a moment when a thought came to her. What if she wrote down a prayer to God as Carrie used to do? Would that help? She thought back to Courtney and the Ladies Fellowship. What would happen if Addie wrote down all the ugly things she had done in her life? Could God really make them beautiful?

God, I'm new at this. I don't even know where to begin.

She paused a moment, thinking.

I guess I should start at the beginning.

Addie thought back as far as she could, to the episode where she stole the gum from the grocery store. She spent the next hour chronicling so many of the bad and ugly things she had done in her lifetime. Page after page filled up with sins she wanted and needed to confess to God. Before she knew it, Addie was at one of the most devastating days of her life; the only problem was that she didn't realize how much she had hurt herself in the process.

God, I had an abortion. I gave no thought to the human life growing inside me. I don't know how You can forgive me for that. I committed murder.

Thinking of Carrie, she added, *Twice.*

Tears escaped her eyes and blurred the ink on the page. All she could do was cry. It was as if her heart was calling out to God, confessing all her sins to Him, and He heard her.

So had her mom.

Addie wasn't exactly sure when, but she realized Mom had come into the room, sat on the bed, and held Addie in her arms as they cried together, Addie sobbing loudly and unashamed. She heard her mother whispering a prayer over her. For the first time in her life, Addie didn't stop her mom from praying. Addie let her mom rock her as if she were a little girl again before she had turned everything in her life sour. Mom's arms were comforting. Perhaps God knew she needed to physically feel being held and sent her mom to take care of that task.

Through her tears, she sobbed out the words that were on her heart. "I've been such a jerk to everyone since I was a little girl. I've done so many horrible things. Things I can't ever make up for."

"You don't have to make up for anything."

"Mom, I not only killed my sister, I killed my baby." She didn't realize she'd said the words until they were out of her mouth.

"I know. We all had to deal with that."

Addie suddenly pulled back from her mom, the tears still flowing. "How did you know?" She wasn't accusing, as the old Addie would have been.

"Someone at church told me. I didn't want to believe it at first. That was about the time I noticed a deeper rift between you and Carrie. She wouldn't even look at you. I knew something was up and that Carrie probably knew all about it. I guess the kids at school were talking. The daughter of the woman at church came to her instead of spreading the gossip among the other kids."

That made Addie weep even more. People knew? How did they know? As far as Addie knew, Carrie was the only one who knew about her and Todd, but she wouldn't have said anything. But then Addie hadn't told Carrie about the abortion, and somehow she had known anyway. How did she find out? That wasn't something Addie thought about at the time because she was so self-absorbed.

"Why didn't you say anything?"

Mom shrugged her shoulders. "I figured you would come to us when the time was right."

Then, after another moment, Mom added, "I also knew you needed to confess your sins for yourself. People can point out your mistakes and flaws all day long with no benefit to you. Not until you admit to your own wrongdoings can there be any repentance and forgiveness of sins."

Addie was flabbergasted that at this moment of

confession, there was no malice in Mom's voice, only sadness. She wasn't condemning Addie for the choices she made. Mom was just there. Available. Like she had always been. Why hadn't Addie seen that before?

"I didn't particularly like the idea of you being a mother at sixteen. We would have worked something out, but by the time we heard, it was too late. We do wish you would have come to us first."

No hate. No anger. No cruelty. Just love. Mom exuded love. Another example of Christ in Addie's life.

Addie looked her mother deeply in the eyes as if for the first time. In a raspy whisper, she wept, "I killed my baby!" Addie felt as if someone was punching her in the gut repeatedly.

Addie felt her mom wrap her arms around her again and hold tight. The two of them cried for what seemed like a long time. Addie cried, thinking about all the little love notes God had left her throughout her entire life. Some of those noted had been delivered in the form of people who tried to reach out and show her how good life could be. Notes she had torn up and thrown back in His face without reading. Addie had worked so hard against Him all her life. She felt completely defeated. When her parents forced her to go to church, she had heard stories of people who had hit rock bottom and had nowhere to look but up. Is that where she was now? She knew she had nothing left.

It was dark outside by the time Addie and her mom pulled apart.

When Addie looked up, she saw her father standing in the doorway with tears rolling down his face. "I didn't want to interrupt."

A new barrage of tears began as he walked toward Addie, uncertainly at first, but the look on her face must have given him the signal he needed as he crossed the room in two quick steps and enfolded her in his strong arms, squeezing the life out of her. It hurt but felt good at the same time.

Maybe he was squeezing the death out of her.

When Addie thought she opened her eyes, they opened in yet another flashback. The family was in church. Not Addie's favorite place to be. Every Sunday, there was a fight between Addie and her parents as Addie was too tired, not in the mood, or had some other flimsy excuse she would try to use to get out of going.

"You can stay home if you're dead or dying."

That was a famous quote from Dad on Sunday mornings. Addie tried to play dead or dying some mornings, but he always saw right through her.

A movement to her left forced Addie's focus on the flashback. It was the end of the service and most of the congregation had their heads bowed in prayer. The family was in their usual spot: third pew, left side. Carrie on the end, then Addie, then her parents. Addie always felt this arrangement was on purpose. Addie used to get up and leave the service, pretending she had to go to the bathroom. Then she would spend as much time in the bathroom as she could, skipping as much of the service as possible. After the second time her mom had to come to the bathroom to make her come back, this new seating arrangement started. If Addie tried to get up, Dad would grab hold of her arm and prevent her from rising. Carrie was the second line of defense, as she would put her legs in such a way that made it hard for Addie to get out of the pew quickly.

Before each service, Dad would ask, "Does anyone have to go potty?"

Addie knew he was trying to be funny, but he failed.

This Sunday memory was one Addie remembered well, not because anyone ever brought it up or because she remembered the message from that day, but because Carrie did something good, yet again, and she didn't even care that no one noticed.

From their vantage point on the third row, they could always see who came to the altar to pray, if one had their eyes open that is, which Addie usually did. She didn't understand her need to spy on other people in private spiritual moments. Maybe it was the fact that if her eyes were closed, she gave others the impression she was praying. Again, no one would notice unless they had their eyes open.

This day, Addie felt Carrie get up and move toward the

front of the church. Addie watched as Carrie knelt next to a woman Carrie babysat for from time to time. Carrie put her arm around the woman, and while Addie could not hear what Carrie was saying, she could see Carrie whispering to the woman and then the two of them bowed their heads while Carrie prayed. Addie couldn't take her eyes off Carrie. She felt anger and resentment building up inside her against her sister. Why did Carrie always have to do the right thing?

Addie glanced to her left when Carrie sat back down next to her, but Carrie already had her head bowed and eyes closed. No one but the three of them knew what Carrie had done. Addie wasn't sure why it rubbed her the wrong way, but it did.

"Maybe it's the Holy Spirit inside other people that you can't handle," Dad had said one Sunday morning when Addie didn't feel like going to church.

Was that what she was feeling now?

Whatever it was, it was aggravating. Addie found it even more infuriating that Carrie didn't care that no one knew when she performed one of her good deeds.

"She has a quiet testimony," Addie had overheard her mother say of Carrie one day. What was that supposed to mean anyway? Addie thought Carrie was loud in her feelings about living a godly life. At least she was at home to Addie.

Maybe that was because Carrie felt Addie needed to hear it more.

Chapter Twenty-Three

It was her twenty-first birthday. And oh, what fun it had been! While Mom and Dad had wanted to do something special with her, she had refused. In the last year she had lived on her own, she had so thoroughly enjoyed the freedom. Addie did what she wanted when she wanted. There was no one to tell her she wasn't doing something right. Carrie's shadow wasn't there to live in. At least all the time. For some reason, that shadow seemed to follow Addie wherever she went, and it made an appearance from time to time.

While drinking wasn't a new habit for Addie, it was now legal, and she had taken advantage of that. She and a couple of friends had visited a few bars and accepted entirely too many drinks from admiring men. By the end of the evening, even Addie knew she'd had too much. Her friends weren't any better, but they still drove away. Addie knew she needed a ride but didn't know who to call.

Carrie.

"Why does her name always pop into my head?" It

exasperated her. However, her other options weren't looking any better. Sighing, she pulled out her phone and sent her sister a text, knowing Carrie would answer because she couldn't help herself.

Dlfeiaheoimpot aelkn elknkl.

What?

Dkeihlkj;oin. *Addie thought she was typing in something that made sense. At least it made sense to her. Apparently, Carrie understood.*

Have you been drinking?

After some more illegible texts, Carrie called.

"Where are you?"

"Bar."

"That doesn't narrow it down."

"Ummm...B..b...Bottom Dollar."

Carrie sighed. "I'll be there in a few."

The first thing Addie heard when Carrie arrived was, "You better not barf in my car."

Addie fell into the passenger seat, and when she shut the door, her face automatically plastered itself against the window. There wasn't too much more of that night she remembered. When she stumbled out of her bedroom the next morning, Carrie was sleeping on her couch.

Addie gave her a shove with her foot. "What are you still doing here?"

Carrie groggily sat up. Pushing her hair out of the way. "We need to talk."

"Have I told you I have a headache?" Addie wasn't any nicer of a person when she had a hangover.

"Do I look like I care? You call me in the middle of the night. I could have told you to call Mom and Dad."

"What do you want?"

"I want you to start acting like an adult. You can't go around acting like an irresponsible teenager for the rest of your life, you know."

"I don't need you to tell me how to live."

Carrie gestured around the disastrous apartment. "Apparently, you do. Did you not pay your electric bill? It's freezing in here, and the heat won't come on. Or the lights. Fortunately, I had a blanket in my car that I could use to cover up with after bringing you home last night. Your kitchen sink is full of moldy dishes. I'd be surprised if you have any clean clothes. And the smell in here ... it's not good."

"Why don't you just mind your own business?"

"I've hardly spoken to you in the last couple of years. But you sure know who to call when you're in trouble, don't you? I think I have every right to tell you a few things. You need to stop sleeping around. You're going to end up pregnant again or get some disease."

Addie interrupted her with, "I take care of things."

"Even when you're drunk? Do you remember to 'take care of things' then? Or do you take care of things like you did when you were sixteen?" Carrie's tone of voice demanded an answer.

But Addie didn't want to give one. She was seething.

"If Mom and Dad knew about half the stuff you do, they would be so disappointed in you."

Addie let out a derisive laugh. "Ha! Like they aren't already? You're the perfect one. You're the one that always makes the right choices. You're the one everyone thinks is so sweet and kind and ... blech! That makes me want to barf more than this hangover."

Carrie just stood there looking at Addie. Shaking her head, she said, "You're pathetic."

"You can leave now."

Carrie grabbed the couple of things she had brought in with her and headed toward the door.

"And don't come back ever again!"

Carrie turned around and said in a much quieter tone of voice, "Surely, you don't mean that."

"Oh, but I do. I don't care if I never see your perfect face again!"

Carrie looked at her for one moment longer. Addie felt some satisfaction by the tears she could see welling up in Carrie's eyes.

"You know I'm moving across the country tomorrow because of my new teaching job. Maybe you'll get your wish."

"Two thousand miles isn't enough space to put between us."

Carrie left without another word.

"Best of friends, worst of enemies." That was the truth. At least the worst of enemies part.

That was the last time they had spoken to each other.

It had been another interminable night. Addie felt like she had been battling her demons all through the long, dark hours. Whatever it was that had been chasing her wore her out mentally and physically. She was exhausted and didn't feel like getting up in the morning, but she knew sleep was not a respite that was coming soon. Restless, Addie felt the need to get up and move around.

Maybe a hot shower will help. Gathering up clean clothes, Addie found her movements jerky and strange. She dropped everything at least twice before finally stumbling to the bathroom. Turning on the water and allowing it to heat up before getting in, she sat on the toilet seat for a few moments to catch her breath. Looking at her hands, she realized they were shaking.

"What in the world?" This was all new to her.

"Are you okay in there?" Mom knocked on the bathroom door, startling Addie. "I heard a lot of noise and wondered if you fell or something."

"No. I'm just clumsy and dropping everything."

"Do you need anything?"

"Just privacy." Addie must have been starting to feel at least a little better since a snide comment slipped out of her mouth without any thought. Her mother's footsteps moved away from the door.

The shaking started again.

Addie closed her eyes and willed herself to shower, skipping the hair washing to save energy and be done as fast as possible.

Finally, she was clean and fully clothed. Sitting on her bed, she was trying to catch her breath. Her heart was racing, whether from the expended energy showering or from the nightmares she didn't know. Looking around, all she saw was Carrie. Even though Carrie's stuff was still all in boxes, Addie could feel her presence. It was unnerving. She thought again about the friends/enemies thing. That's when the realization hit her. Carrie had always wanted to be the best of friends. They were sisters, after all. Built-in best friends. But Addie had only ever made them the worst of enemies.

"I have to get out of this house."

A thought suddenly came to her. Would her mom notice if she took the car? First, Addie would have to force the tremors in her hands to stop or driving would be tedious at least. But Addie wanted to get away. Far away. And not come back.

Making her way slowly down the stairs to try and calm herself down, she came up with a plan.

"I'm going to get outside to get some air."

"It's a perfect day to sit outside. I can bring a comfier chair out to the porch."

"No. I need to move, to breathe, to get away from these four walls for a little bit. I think I'll take a little walk."

Mom looked down at Addie's hands which were still shaking some.

"Are you sure?"

Addie knew her mom had a hard time trusting her.

Keep cool.

"Yeah, I'm sure."

"Well, I guess it's okay. Do you want me to go with you?"

Addie shook her head. "No." Feeling she responded too quickly, she added, "But thanks."

That must have made her mom feel a little better as she smiled and put her hand on Addie's arm. "Just be careful. If you feel yourself getting too tired, make sure to turn around and come back."

It was like Addie wasn't an adult and had never taken a walk before. "I won't be long," Addie lied as she headed out the door. She snuck the keys from the hook by the front door, trying to keep them from jangling.

First, Addie picked up the ignition interlock. She had seen her mom use it several times, so Addie followed those steps. As soon as it beeped, Addie inserted the key but didn't start the car just yet. Remembering all the times she had snuck away in the middle of the night with the car when she was a teenager, she applied all the tactics, such as not fully closing the door tightly and popping the clutch so she could back down the driveway without a sound. Before leaving the driveway, she took note of how much gas was in the car. The tank was full, so she figured she could get at least five hundred miles away. It wasn't far enough, she thought, but she wasn't sure there was a planet in the galaxy that was far enough to get out from under the presence of Carrie.

Addie looked behind her as she pulled away from the house, half expecting to see her mom running down the driveway, waving her hands for Addie to stop. But no one was there. Addie was in the clear, and freedom awaited her.

Just as she was pulling onto the highway to head out of town as fast as she could, she started to smell something strange. Then she saw several lights on the dashboard flash with urgency and smoke start pouring out from under the hood, so thick, it blocked her vision. The smell of something hot, like burning oil, assaulted her nostrils. Addie held her breath to keep it from entering her lungs. Sighing, she pulled over to the side of the road. This was not what she had planned for the day. Ten miles. That's as far as she managed to get away. She was a loser at running away, too.

After turning on the hazard lights, she pulled out her phone and thought about who she could call. She could call her mom, but Mom was part of what she was running away from and Mom also had no car at the moment. She could call a tow truck, but that would require a credit card, which she didn't have. It didn't take her long to scroll through her contacts. Dad. Mom. That was it. She laid her head back on the seat in frustration.

A knocking on her window startled her heart to racing. Something chased her down while she was trying to sleep, and people chased her down when she was awake.

An audible sigh of disappointment escaped her when she saw who was standing there. She let out a sigh of disappointment as she rolled down the window.

"Of all the days I choose to be a Good Samaritan, you're the one."

"I'm not exactly happy about it either, Colin." She spit out his name as if it tasted bad.

"I didn't think you were supposed to be driving."

"Are you pretending to be Officer Sanders now?"

"Pop the hood."

Addie did as he demanded.

After a few moments, he came back to the window. "You aren't going anywhere. It looks like the radiator is cracked. Call a tow truck, and I'll take you home."

"I'll be fine. I can walk."

Colin tilted his head and smirked at her. He knew she would never be able to walk the ten miles home on her own.

"Fine." Addie called a tow truck and then called her mom with the information so she could pay for it. An awkward silence reigned while they waited.

Once the tow truck pulled away with the car, Colin opened the passenger side door of his car and waved her in without saying a word.

Grudgingly, Addie got in. After her door closed, it seemed like Coin was taking a while to get in the driver's side. Addie looked in the side-view mirror and saw him talking on the phone. Apparently, it was a private conversation and not one he wanted her to hear. Whatever.

"So, aren't you a little old to be running away from home?" Colin asked as he flopped down in his seat.

"We don't have to talk, you know."

"Oh, I know! But God has you in my car for a reason. If I had known it was you on the side of the road, I would have kept on driving. But unfortunately for me, God didn't tell me who was waiting."

"You could have. I wasn't forcing you to help me. I didn't even ask for your help."

Colin didn't say anything at first. Addie could tell he was angry because she could see his jaw muscles twitch as he ground his teeth, much like her father usually did when he was frustrated with her. Finally, he spoke. "I didn't walk away because of Carrie. Carrie would never have turned someone down who needed help."

"Oh, please! Just what I want to hear more about today—how good Carrie was. Maybe we need to get some new bracelets—WWCD—what would Carrie do?"

More teeth grinding. It made Addie feel good that she knew how to push his buttons.

"God has a way of working things out the way He wants, not the way we want."

Addie was having a bad enough day; she didn't need to hear about God.

"I know why you were so rude to me in the hospital."

"Oh, you do, do you?"

"I was hurt. You could kick me because I was down. You can't handle me in my normal, healthy self."

"Ha!" His laugh wasn't really a laugh. "That's why you think I gave you the cold shoulder in the hospital?"

"Yeah."

"It had nothing to do with anything else?"

"Nope."

His voice was quiet and controlled when he spoke next. "You know, your sister always saw me as a person."

Addie tried to interrupt him with a snarky comment, but Colin held up his hand authoritatively, and Addie couldn't help but not speak. Immediately, she pressed her lips together to compel herself to be silent.

"She saw me as a person. I think it was our first day of kindergarten when she reached out to me. That was the first time I felt someone cared. My parents certainly didn't. All through school, Carrie was there for me, not only in the bad times but in the good. She cheered me on when I was successful. She pulled me up every time I felt down. She's the one who told me there was Someone who loved me more than anyone else could. It was prom night when she led me to the Lord. It wasn't just because of the words she said; it was the way she chose to live her life. Nothing about her was fake. She was the same no matter who she was with.

"We would often take the time to pray together. If I had a specific worry, she would always remember to ask me about it. We prayed together about you. She loved you, you know. There is nothing she wouldn't have done for you. Carrie just wanted to see you turn your life around and live for the Lord. She always quoted the verse about life being a vapor. Life is too short not to live each day to the fullest. And she did exactly that.

"Over the last couple years of our dating relationship—which you knew absolutely nothing about—she taught me that I needed to forgive you for how you treated me. It was hard. I was almost there before the accident happened."

After this revelation, he stopped for a moment. Addie knew she would get the hand again if she tried to speak, so she simply acted as if she was barely listening. A yawn punctuated her outward appearance, but her insides felt like they were tearing apart. It felt as if some creature had jabbed its claws into her chest and ripped her heart in two before pulling it out.

"The icing on the cake was when you came onto my ward, and I had to take care of you. I have never felt such temptation to end a life as I did when I saw your face. You are such an ugly person on the inside, and I didn't care what happened to you."

Addie's thoughts went back to the comment Carrie had made about her artwork being a representation of who she was in her heart. Then Courtney and her ugly quilt pieces came to Addie's mind. Was she truly an ugly person? All she ever wanted was for someone to love her. And no one did, except for Grandma Marjie.

Through his tears, Colin continued. "You killed one of the most precious people in this world. She was everything to me. She was my life. After I heard she was gone, I didn't care if I lived or died. I felt that death would be better."

He pulled into her parents' driveway. Taking a deep, shuddering breath, he said, "There, I brought you home. My good deed for the day is done. Get out of my car."

Addie didn't need to hear that twice. But before she slammed the door in anger, he called out to her once more.

"Addie." He took a deep breath before continuing as if he was about to utter the hardest words of his life. Addie stood straight, not bending down to look at him in the car. "I forgive you."

Shocked, Addie had no response, and she no longer felt the desire to slam the door. All of a sudden, she didn't feel she had the strength for that. Slowly, she stumbled up to the house.

Mom met her at the door. "Are you okay? I'm sorry you had car trouble. You should have told me you wanted to drive."

"I'm fine." Addie knew she couldn't talk to her mom without crying. "I'm tired. I'm going to my room."

As she trudged up the stairs, her mom said, "We'll talk about this later."

And Addie knew they would, but she raised her hand to show she had heard but didn't say another word. She couldn't. She also couldn't take this back and forth of her emotions anymore. Could she really and truly change or not? Did she want to?

In her room, she lay down on the bed, curled up in the fetal position, and sobbed into the pillow she'd scrunched up beneath her head. Not only was she upset about her interaction with Colin, but also because she knew she had messed up ... again. Why could she never choose to do the right thing? Why could she not be more like Carrie and just be good? Addie sobbed herself to sleep.

The next day, Addie had another meeting with Pastor Townsend. "What's the point if I'm going to constantly fail anyway? That's what I'm good at. Maybe I should stick to that."

After she spilled her guts about what she had done, how she was a failure, was unlovable, and how she wanted to even stop trying, Pastor Townsend did give her a bit of encouragement.

"No one is perfect. No one makes the right decisions all the time. We all fail daily. God knew all the choices we would make before we were even a blip on anyone's radar. He always knows, but He still loves us. God had a purpose for Carrie, and God has a purpose for you. Your purposes are not the same, and you need to realize that and stop trying to be like her. If God wanted two Carries, He would have made two, but He didn't. He created a girl named Caroline and a girl named Adeline. They are two completely different people, with two completely different purposes."

He paused for a moment. Leaning forward with his elbows on his knees and his hands clasped in front of him, he caught Addie's eyes and held them.

"Have you ever realized that you're sabotaging yourself trying to be like someone else? You will never be what or who anyone else is, no matter how hard you try, because you weren't meant to be like them. So how about you just start trying to be the Addie God created you to be? God has plans for you, and until you fulfill those plans, He will keep you from destroying yourself."

That left Addie with much to think about.

Chapter Twenty-Four

The dreams. Would they haunt her forever? Again, she found herself pursued. She didn't know who it was or why they were chasing her. Somehow, Addie knew the pursuer wasn't running briskly after her but following at a slow and steady pace, one that wouldn't make her breathe so hard. In spite of the fact that she was running and out of breath and he was walking, he was always right behind her or right in front of her or right beside her. Close. She knew it was a man, but in her dreams, she couldn't think of anyone who would follow after her and call to her so intently and deliberately. Not to mention so constantly and for so long. None of the men she knew outside her dreams pursued her for much of anything for any length of time.

"Addie, please come to me."

The voice wasn't demanding. It wasn't frightening, yet it still scared her. Perhaps if she knew who it was, she could have stopped running, sat, and had a chat.

"I know what you've done."

Now that absolutely scared her! There were things she'd done that no one knew about. Not her parents. Not her friends, not that she had many. Not even Carrie. At least she didn't think Carrie had known about them, but then again ...

Images of Carrie fluttered through her mind, quickly coming and going. There were so many; most of them were not good ones. Most of them were memories where Addie had done something to upset Carrie or hurt her feelings. Addie was beginning to feel something she'd never felt before. What was that? Remorse? She began to feel almost sorry for some of the things she had done to Carrie over the years. Sorry for some of the things she'd done to other people as well.

"I love you."

There was the voice again. Why did it keep hunting her down? Love was not something she could ever remember feeling. No love to her from others and definitely no love from her to others. Who could love her? Someone so broken.

Addie began crying. She wept uncontrollably. Addie never used to cry before, but she seemed to do it a lot lately. She always put on a big show of not caring. Now ... she was starting to care. Finally, out of breath and not feeling that she could run another step, she came to a door. While she had been inside this same time of dream multiple times, she had never gone through this door. Although she had seen it before, for some reason, she had ignored it. It was in plain *sight but not ostentatious. It was subdued. Wondering why she had never paid attention to it before, she took a deep breath and opened it.*

Addie woke up with a start. The sky outside the window was pitch black. It was still night. In her dream she had been crying, and now she noticed the dampness on her pillow that told her she had been crying in real life as well.

Her hand hit something as she moved to sit up. Turning on the light, she saw a sketchbook and a box of colored pencils. Her mom must have left it there as some sort of peace offering about the whole taking the car without permission or a license thing. She picked it up and opened the cover of the sketchbook. There was something about a new sketchbook. The smell. It filled Addie's soul. She opened the box of pencils. A different smell that had the same type of feeling. Brushing her hand over the first page of the sketchbook, a picture started forming in her mind. Grabbing the black pencil, she began to sketch it out. Tilting her head to the side and sticking her tongue out of the corner of her mouth, she observed what she had started. It was dark. It was desolate. This dismal style seemed to be the pictures from her mind when she had those nightmares that frightened her so much. It was scary. It suddenly held no appeal for her to finish it. It didn't feel right anymore. It didn't appeal to her. What was the matter? She tore out the sheet, crumpled it up, and threw it toward the garbage can.

Shaking her head, Addie moved on and grabbed another pencil, one with color. Remembering what her art teacher used to say about allowing the work to just come, Addie started moving the pencil around on the page with no particular picture in mind. It was a little crude at first; it had been a while since she tried to draw, but eventually, a sunflower started forming on the page as well as a smile on her face. Sunflowers always reminded her of Grandma Marjie. Grandma Marjie had sunflowers in her kitchen wallpaper. The more Addie thought about that wallpaper, the more she realized that was what was coming out onto the page—Grandma Marjie's kitchen wallpaper.

Then, a new thought came to her mind. Addie got up out of bed to get Carrie's Bible. Holding the spine with her legs, Addie placed her thumbs in the middle of the closed pages. Wherever she opened up to, she would find something else beautiful to draw. The pages landed flat on her lap as Carrie's Bible was well used, and the spine had long ago lost its stiffness. Carrie had highlighted Psalm 23 in green, and it caught Addie's eye. Addie read the words, not really thinking about them much. Then she flipped the sketchbook to a new page and picked out one of the green colored pencils. She had no idea how long she worked, but she ended up with a pastoral picture. It was of a shepherd surrounded by sheep in a field sprinkled with daisies. It was bright. It was colorful. It was beautiful. It was nothing like her.

Realization hit her and hit her hard. Again, she started to cry. It was all too much. Seeing Colin and hearing what he said. What her parents and sister had tried to tell her over the years. The accident. The dreams. The realization coming from her drawing.

She repeated one phrase over and over again. "God, I need You!" It seemed like hours that she cried out to God. There weren't many different words coming out of her heart, just the tears and an understanding of need.

When she noticed she had stopped crying, the sunlight was pouring through the room. Sitting up and looking out the window, she realized it was morning, and her eyes were dry. Apparently, she had fallen asleep in her tears and anguish and had awoken feeling refreshed and renewed. Dreams of someone chasing her had not continued to haunt her throughout the remainder of the night. She had, for once in as long as she could remember, slept peacefully.

Looking over to the nightstand, she saw the

pastoral picture she had drawn during the night. It was still early, but she carefully ripped out the page and tiptoed down the stairs so her parents would not hear her. She placed that picture on the table right where she knew her mom and dad would see it first thing in the morning.

∞ ∞ ∞

Can you meet me at the coffee shop close to my house at seven tonight? Addie texted.

Why?

At least Colin responded. That was already more than what Addie had hoped for. *We need to talk. At least I need to talk.*

It took several minutes before Colin answered. Addie could almost feel the struggle he had debating on whether he should or not.

I'll give you fifteen minutes.

That was also more than Addie had hoped for.

Later that evening, there were butterflies in Addie's stomach as she waited for Colin. She had arrived a little early because she needed to prepare herself for what she had to say. She also wanted to be able to take a few seconds to compose herself when she saw him coming.

After she saw Colin's car pull up and park, Addie

watched him get out, bypass the coffee counter, sit at the table with her, and stare her down. He was still in his scrubs, so he must have come straight from work.

"I thought you said you forgave me that day when you rescued me." Addie knew she had to be careful not to let the old Addie rear her ugly head, but sarcasm was second nature.

"I did, but I never said I wanted to be friends."

Fair enough.

Addie took a deep breath and then said what she had come to say, "I know you said you forgave me, but I wanted to apologize. I'm sorry for all the mean things I said and did to you while we were growing up. I'm sorry I never gave you the respect you deserved. I'm sorry I never treated you the way Carrie did. I'm sorry. For everything."

Addie felt as if she were shrinking because of the way Colin was glaring at her. She hadn't been sure he would be receptive of her apology, but now that seemed apparent. Addie returned his stare, waiting for him to say something. Anything.

"I'm also sorry that I stole a life with Carrie away from you." That was the hardest thing she had to say.

His eyes twitched as if he were trying to control his rage or his desire to cry. Maybe it was both.

After a few moments that seemed endless, Addie gathered up her purse and cup of coffee. "I'm sorry I asked you to come."

She hadn't passed all the way by Colin when he reached out and grabbed her arm.

"I said I forgive you, and I do. It's just hard. Forgive me. I'm still a work in progress as far as God is concerned."

Addie slipped him a little bit of a shy smile. "Yeah. Me too." Then she left.

On the walk home, she went through the scene several times in her head. At first, she wondered what she had done wrong, but then she realized she hadn't done anything wrong. She and Colin were sinners in whom God was still working. They weren't perfect. She understood Colin's need for time and distance from the situation and from her. They would never be close friends, and that was okay. Addie did what she needed to do by asking his forgiveness. Colin had done what he needed to do by accepting her apology. They didn't become enemies overnight. They wouldn't become friends that way either. Addie knew in this regard her conscience was clear. And that's what mattered.

When she got home, her parents were out. Having no idea how long they would be, Addie grabbed a bottle of water and went to her room. She was exhausted. Apologizing was tiring. As she passed through the living room, she noticed something new hanging on the wall. Stopping to take a closer look, she saw that it was her pastoral picture. Tears that seemed to come so easily lately rolled down her cheeks. Mom had the picture framed.

Maybe they didn't hate her after all.

∞ ∞ ∞

Addie thought back on all the dreams she'd had since the accident. She wasn't sure she could trust her memories anymore. Were they factual, or were they distorted, the way she wanted to remember things? Maybe her thoughts were skewed right from the start.

Dad had bought her a journal that he said reminded him of her. She had been writing in the one she had bought so much that it was almost full. Dad had noticed and purchased another. This one had an intricate cover with a lot of detail.

"The more you look at it, the more there is to see. Just like you," Dad had said.

Now Addie pulled out that journal and decided to write her dreams in it, at least what she could remember. The more she wrote down, the more she questioned her memories, even though she seemed to have very clear pictures in her head. She had often heard of people having repressed memories or not remembering things as they really happened, and Addie always thought it was a farce. People remembered what happened to them. But did they? Did they remember situations correctly or were they too caught up in emotions to remember properly? Had Addie been too steeped in her hatred to see reality and saw only what she wanted to see? How was she going to figure this out? Asking her parents was out of the question. They had their own points of view that might be out of sorts, too.

Words Carrie had once said came to Addie's mind. "Ask God. He'll tell you."

Would He? She knew He couldn't lie. So Addie prayed. She prayed that God would open her eyes to see what was true and what was not.

In the midst of her prayer, the colored pencil dream came to her mind, and her eyes popped open. Why that one? Closing her eyes again and trying to focus her thoughts on what God was trying to tell her, she tried to remember every detail of that day.

She was angry; she definitely remembered that. Mom had been crying all day, which put Addie out of sorts even more than she usually was. Grandma Marjie and Papa Forest. That's when it hit her. That was the day they received the news about the accident. That was the day Addie's world fell apart. That was the day she thought she had no one left in the world who loved her. She was mad that the accident had taken away the only people that seemed to get her. Addie had been too little at the time to vocalize her raging feelings. They just came out as hatred. And had kept coming out that way ever since.

She bowed her head again.

"God, please take all this hatred from my heart. I don't want to be like this anymore. It's exhausting. I want to feel free. I want to enjoy life. I want to have fun with people around me. I want to have friends. I want to love only You, and I want that love to show through me as it did through Carrie."

She began writing some more. The scary dreams of someone chasing her came to mind. She tried to recall as much detail as she could from those, even though she didn't think they were real memories. As she wrote, she realized there had been no reason to fear. No one had been chasing her at all. It was God who had been calling to her. While there were some days Addie thought she had been running away from Carrie, she now realized it wasn't Carrie Addie had been running from but the Holy Spirit that lived inside her sister. She had been running because she was afraid to open herself up to God and allow Him to see what an ugly mess she had become. Something deep down inside of her figured God had known what an ugly mess she had become all along. There were no secrets from Him.

God had been inviting her to come into His presence, but she had rejected Him. Repeatedly.

But no more.

A year ago, Addie's life as she knew it had come to a crashing halt. It had been a long road to recovery; however, slowly but surely, Addie was gaining strength and able to do much of what she used to do physically. At least all the good and beneficial things. Her life had changed drastically. No longer did she wake up every morning wondering how she could terrorize those she didn't like. She even picked up some of the slack at her parents' house. Not only that, she was starting her own business, with the financial help of her parents.

Over the last six months, Addie had turned trash into treasures. She had made a pretty penny on the furniture pieces she had restored to new life. It had become symbolic of her life with Christ. She had some rough spots; she even still had some brokenness within her, but God was helping her to work through all that. God was making her into something new. Pastor Townsend and she still met regularly. As he had told her before, things didn't happen overnight, and problems wouldn't be solved overnight. But she was improving daily; she could feel it. Addie had done everything the court required to get her license back and would have that little card that gave her permission to drive in her hand in the next week or so. She didn't even mind that she had to have an ignition interlock when she got a car. It would prove she was truly trying to change.

Maybe soon, life would be back to normal. But then again, she didn't want to go back to the normal of her old life. Addie wanted all things to become new.

Business had not quite become good enough for her to move out of her parents' house and back into her own apartment yet, but it would come. Addie didn't hate being there now. In fact, her dad was her biggest supporter of her new business. He would purposely drive around neighborhoods wherever he happened to be and load up his truck with all kinds of furniture for Addie to refinish or repaint.

"This is amazing!" Mom had said one day while admiring a sofa table. Addie had painted a ring of flowers around the top edge. "I'm glad you left some of the scars. They make it even more beautiful, just like you."

Addie wasn't sure how to respond. She never felt like she had been complimented for much in her life. Of course, now she knew she hadn't done much that was worthy of complimenting. But all that would change. She certainly had plenty of scars, but she would take a page out of Carrie's books and meet people where they were. Perhaps she could reach people others couldn't because of shared experiences.

She fingered the brooch that now hung on a slim, gold chain around her neck. She had tried to give it back to her mom after explaining what she did and what she found with the hidden brooch.

"Carrie must have wanted you to have it if she knew it was there and left it. Stuff was never important to her. But you always were."

So, Addie had bought a petite chain that fit through one of the holes around the edge of the brooch and wore it daily to remind her that, yes, she had made mistakes, but God is greater than any mistake she had ever made and so was His forgiveness. She wore it to remind her of Carrie and to keep her sister close to her heart.

Soon, she would open a storefront in the village where she could sell her art and salvaged items or work on special pieces customers asked her to do. A couple of her favorite framed artwork pieces only contained words. They were the words of the verses Pastor Townsend had given her when he first came to counsel her. Even though she had thrown away the cards as soon as he left, somehow, they were stuck in her memory. These were some of her favorite pieces, and she wasn't exactly sure she was going to sell them. Maybe she would just hang them on the wall behind the counter at the store and use them as witnessing tools whenever anyone asked about them.

It had taken her a little while to come up with a name for her business: Within the 'Lines. This was a play on their names – Adeline and Caroline as well as a reminder that the Holy Spirit of God was now living within her as He had in Carrie. It was different than anything Addie had ever experienced in her life, and she was grateful to God, not to mention Carrie, for giving her a second chance at life. Addie didn't know where she would be without either of them. Well, she vaguely knew—not here on earth, and certainly not in heaven.

Spring was a time of new beginnings. March had rolled around again, and Addie had chosen March 15th, the anniversary of the accident, as the day to open her new store. She needed to recognize that date as something new and beautiful. Addie didn't want to flip the calendar over to March every single year and be reminded of the horrible thing she had done. She needed the day to be a celebration. It was a day that big changes in her life began. No, she would never forget, but she knew God and her parents had forgiven her. Spring was a time when all that appeared dead suddenly looked vibrant and full of life. And Addie had never felt more full of life than she did now.

Addie became a member of the choir in church. She had never known she could sing well, until she actually started singing. It pained her to think how well hers and Carrie's voices would have harmonized had they both been there. Addie didn't walk around as if her life were a musical like Carrie did, but there was definitely a song on her heart more often than not now.

Pictures of Carrie singing in church often came to Addie's mind. Yes, Carrie had a beautiful voice, but it wasn't her voice that Addie remembered the most. It was her face. It was otherworldly while she was singing. Shining. It was as if Carrie was in the presence of God when she sang His praises. Now she truly was.

One Sunday morning at church, Addie had taken those steps out of the pew, not to hide out in the bathroom, but to walk to the front of the church where the altar was. There she had knelt down and prayed a prayer she never thought she would utter.

"God, I'm sorry. I'm sorry for all the things I've done. I don't think I need to list them again, as we both know what they are. I thank You for blessing me with a sister like Carrie, who lived her life for You. She was a walking testament of Your love for me. She showed it to me every day in spite of the way I treated her. Lord, please forgive me. I know I need You in my life. I want You in my life. I want to be different, and I know You are the only One that can make that happen. Come into my life today and change me. I am in desperate need of a Savior. I promise to live for You just as Carrie did. With every breath."

Dear Reader,

Have you ever thought you were too far out of God's reach for Him to love you? Have you ever thought that the bad things you've done would prevent God from loving you? If you have thought these things, I want you to know that you are wrong. God created you. He has loved you since before the creation of the world.

If you feel this way, please find someone to talk to who can lead you through the Scriptures and show you the truth. If you don't have anyone, please feel free to send me an email at oneilruth@gmail.com.

Know that God as always loved you and always will.

About the Author

Ruth O'Neil has been a freelance writer for 30-plus years. She sees everything as a writing opportunity in disguise, whether it is an interesting character, setting, or situation. You can find her book series "What a Difference a Year Makes" and other books at most online retailers as well as her website (http://ruthoneilauthor.com/). When she's not writing or teaching the next generation of writers, Ruth spends her time quilting, reading, scrapbooking, camping and spending time with her family.

www.ingramcontent.com/pod-product-compliance
Lightning Source LLC
Chambersburg PA
CBHW030930260626
47169CB00002B/428